CHARLES DICKENS'S

A CHRISTMAS CAROL

A GRAPHIC NOVEL

BY BENJAMIN HARPER &
DONO SANCHEZ-ALMARA

STONE ARCH BOOKS
A CAPSTONE IMPRINT

Graphic Revolve is published by Stone Arch Books
A Capstone Imprint
1710 Roe Crest Drive, North Mankato, Minnesota 56003
www.capstonepub.com

Cataloging-in-Publication Data is available at the Library
of Congress website.
Hardcover ISBN: 978-1-4965-0370-1
Paperback ISBN: 978-1-4965-0378-7
Ebook PDF ISBN: 978-1-4965-2316-7

Summary: Ebenezer Scrooge has always hated
Christmas, but in this particular Eve, he's given
another reason to be wary of the holiday: the ghost of
Jacob Marley comes to visit! Clad in heavy chains and
burdensome weights, Marley's ghost warns Scrooge that
three spirits will visit him over the next three nights, each
with a ghastly story to share. Will Scrooge's ghoulish
experience teach him to embrace the spirit of Christmas?

Common Core back matter written by Dr. Katie Monnin.

Designer: Alison Thiele

Printed in the United States of America in
North Mankato, Minnesota.
009389R

TABLE OF CONTENTS

A CHRISTMAS CAROL AND CHARITY

Charles Dickens's *A Christmas Carol* was published on December 18th, 1843, in London, England. The novella tells the tale of Ebenezer Scrooge, a bitter old man with no interest in charity or the so-called "holiday spirit" of Christmas. However, Scrooge soon learns the value of charity and kindness — a message Charles Dickens felt was necessary to share during the bleak and poor state of London in his time. Thankfully, the story had several big effects on readers, some of which have spread around the world and continue to this day!

The phrase "Merry Christmas" first became popular after the publication of the story. Ever since, the moniker "Scrooge" and the phrase "Bah humbug!" have become popular labels for those types of people who express dislike of the holidays (or even just for making fun of people with a poor attitude about anything in general).

Less than one year after the publication of *A Christmas Carol*, several important people made charitable donations after being inspired by Dickens's tale. Robert Louis Stevenson, a famous writer, made public vows to give to charities. And in America, a man named Mr. Fairbanks closed his factory on Christmas and sent turkeys to all of his employees in honor of the spirit of the tale. A soldier named Captain Corbett-Smith even told the story to his men between battles in the trenches of World War I.

Some experts have even linked the Western world's modern day Christmas customs of giving and charity to Dickens's tale. Festive feasts, family gatherings, and a general attitude of giving and kindness grew in popularity in response to the positive message of Dickens's story!

CAST OF CHARACTERS

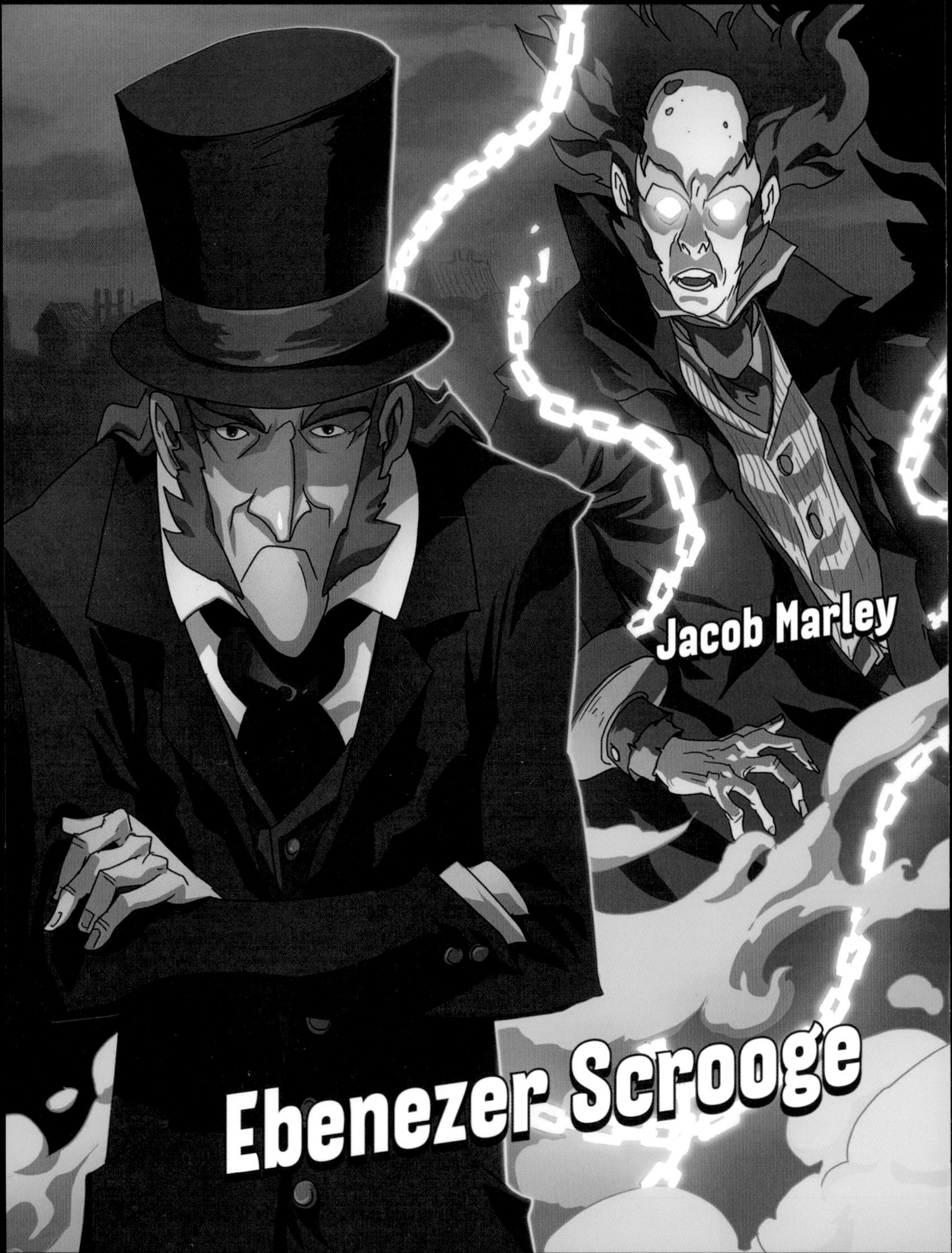
Jacob Marley
Ebenezer Scrooge

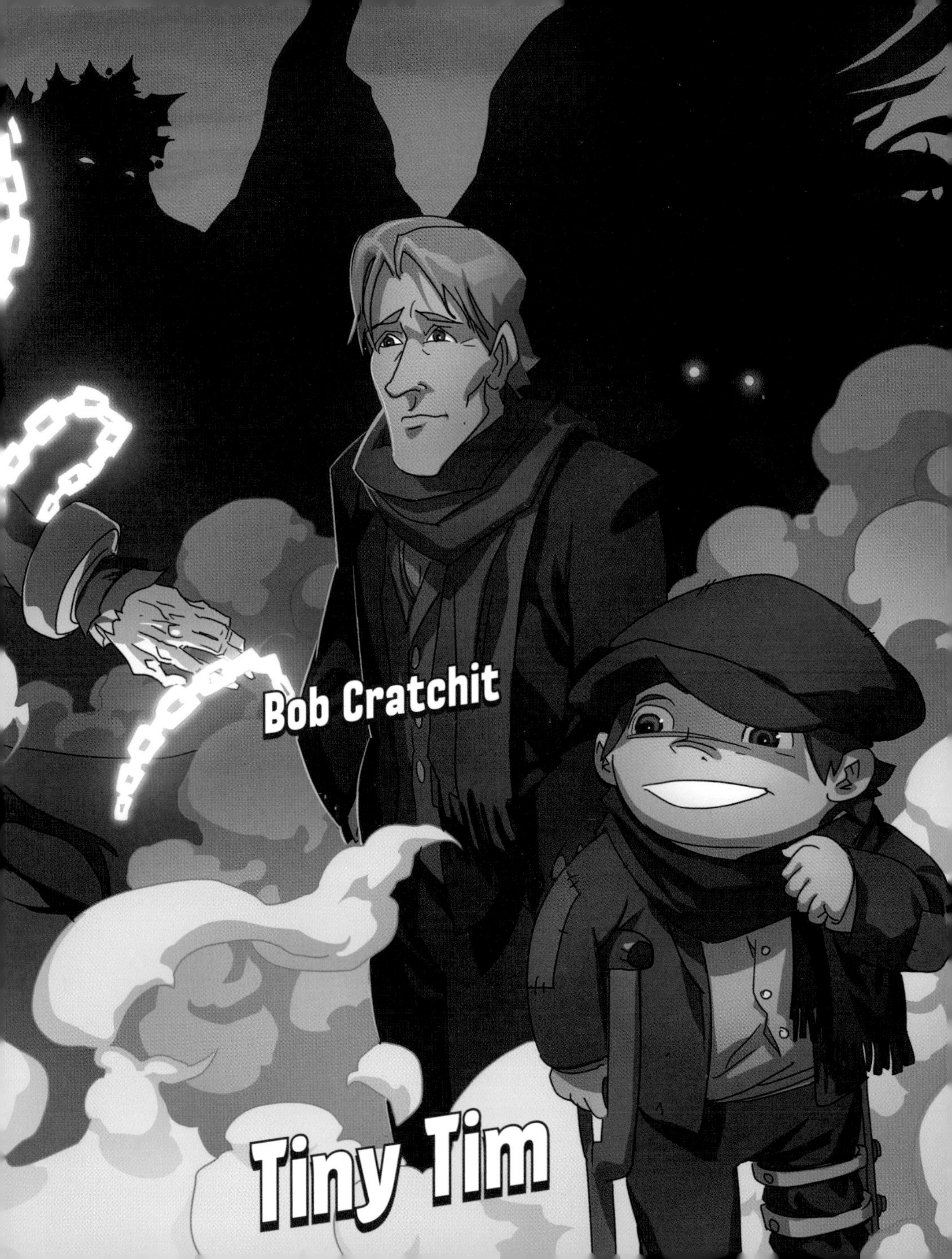
Bob Cratchit
Tiny Tim

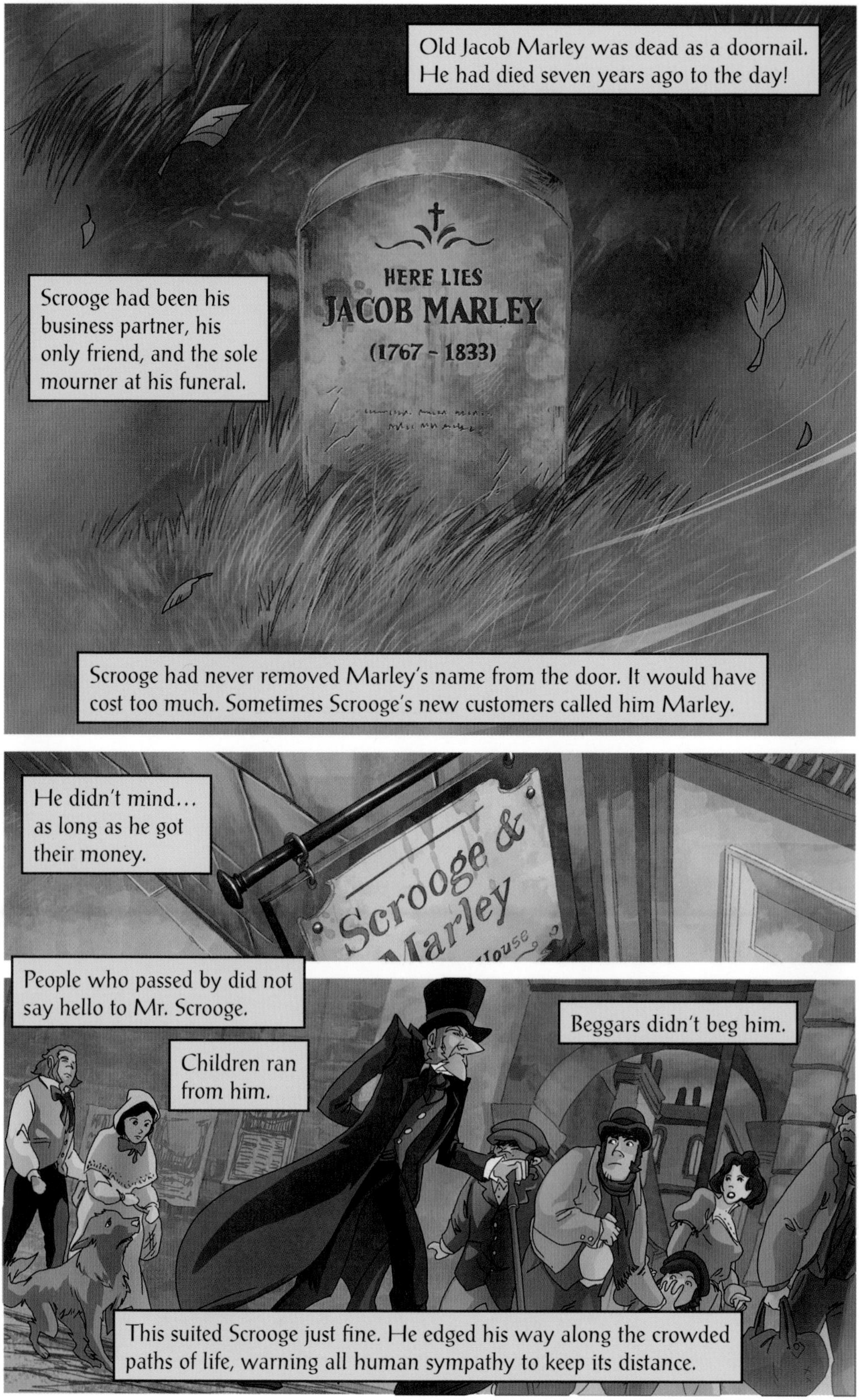
Old Jacob Marley was dead as a doornail. He had died seven years ago to the day!
HERE LIES
JACOB MARLEY
(1767 - 1833)
Scrooge had been his business partner, his only friend, and the sole mourner at his funeral.
Scrooge had never removed Marley's name from the door. It would have cost too much. Sometimes Scrooge's new customers called him Marley.
He didn't mind… as long as he got their money.
Scrooge &
Marley
People who passed by did not say hello to Mr. Scrooge.
Children ran from him.
Beggars didn't beg him.
This suited Scrooge just fine. He edged his way along the crowded paths of life, warning all human sympathy to keep its distance.

CHAPTER 1
CHRISTMAS EVE

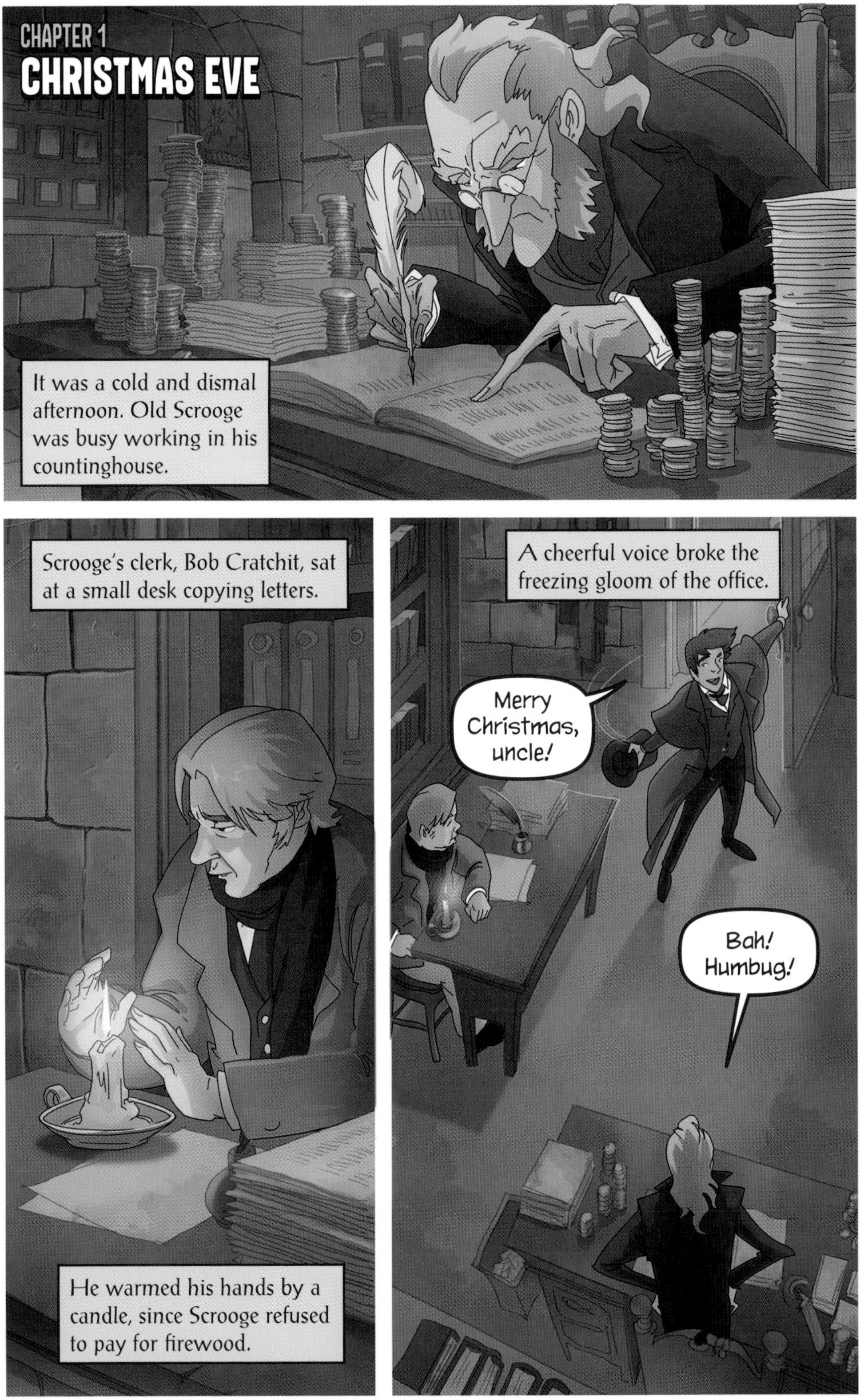
It was a cold and dismal afternoon. Old Scrooge was busy working in his countinghouse.
Scrooge's clerk, Bob Cratchit, sat at a small desk copying letters.
He warmed his hands by a candle, since Scrooge refused to pay for firewood.
A cheerful voice broke the freezing gloom of the office.
Merry Christmas, uncle!
Bah! Humbug!

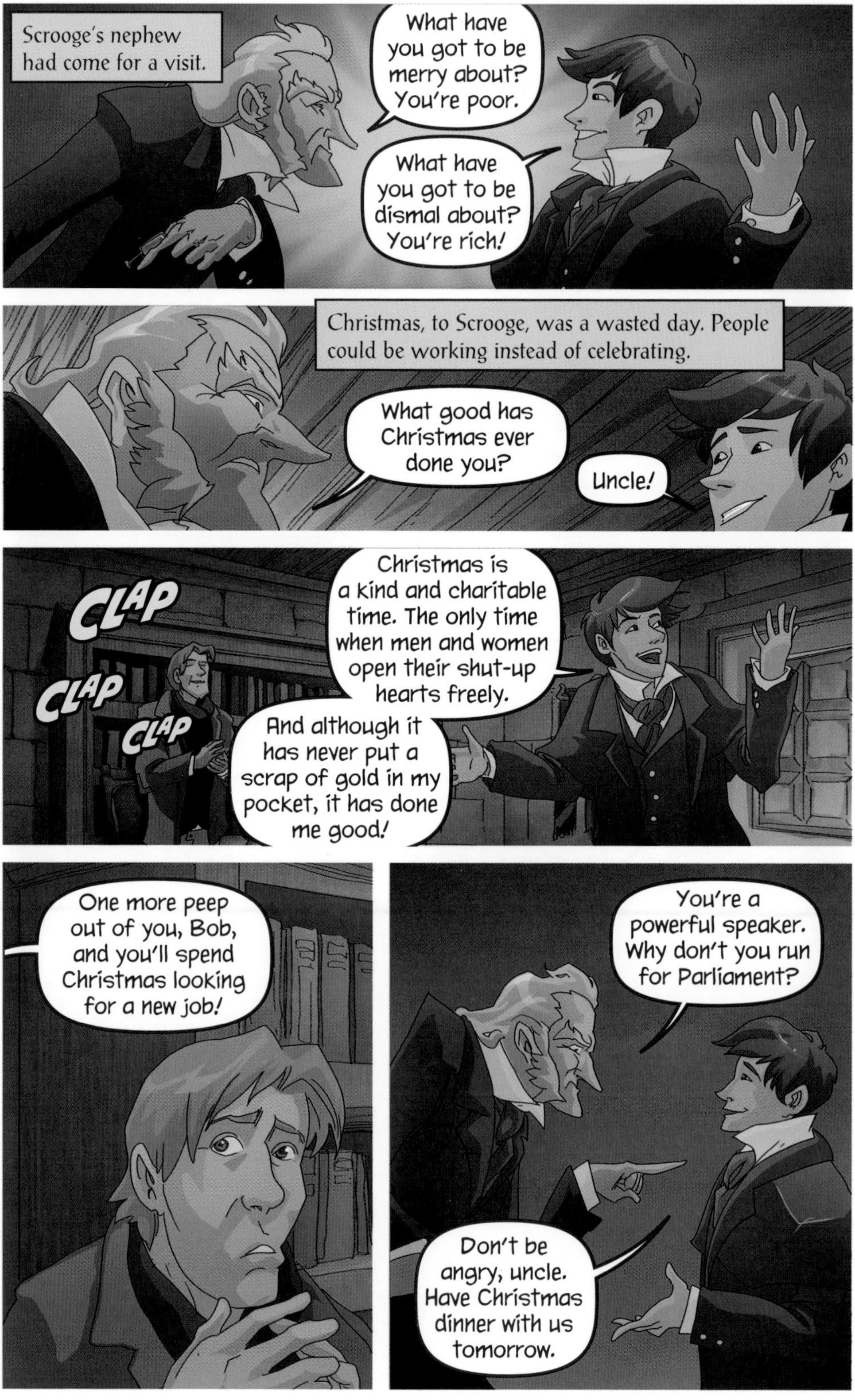
Scrooge's nephew had come for a visit.
What have you got to be merry about? You're poor.
What have you got to be dismal about? You're rich!
Christmas, to Scrooge, was a wasted day. People could be working instead of celebrating.
What good has Christmas ever done you?
Uncle!
Christmas is a kind and charitable time. The only time when men and women open their shut-up hearts freely.
And although it has never put a scrap of gold in my pocket, it has done me good!
CLAP
CLAP
CLAP
One more peep out of you, Bob, and you'll spend Christmas looking for a new job!
You're a powerful speaker. Why don't you run for Parliament?
Don't be angry, uncle. Have Christmas dinner with us tomorrow.

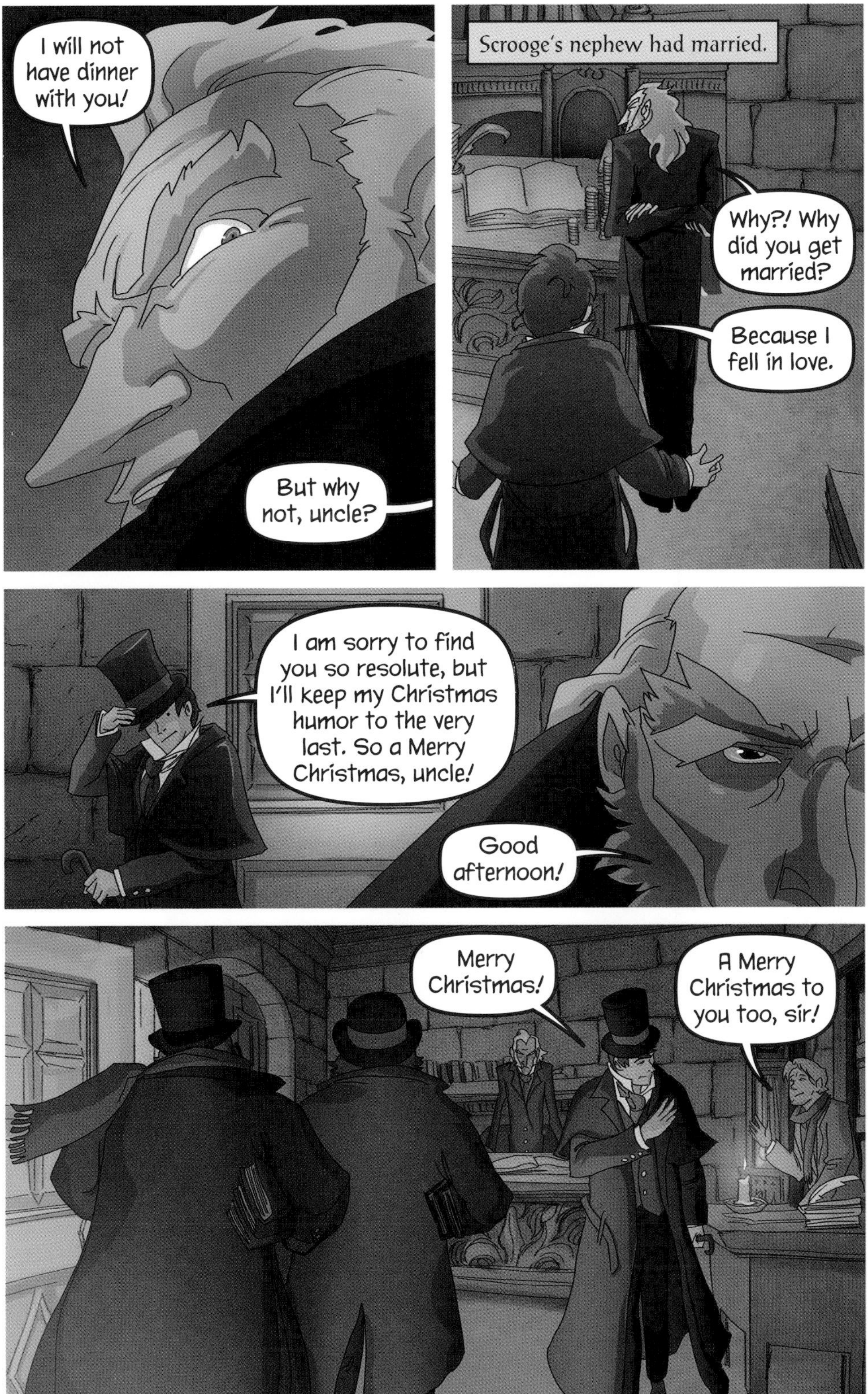
I will not have dinner with you!
But why not, uncle?
Scrooge's nephew had married.
Why?! Why did you get married?
Because I fell in love.
I am sorry to find you so resolute, but I'll keep my Christmas humor to the very last. So a Merry Christmas, uncle!
Good afternoon!
Merry Christmas!
A Merry Christmas to you too, sir!

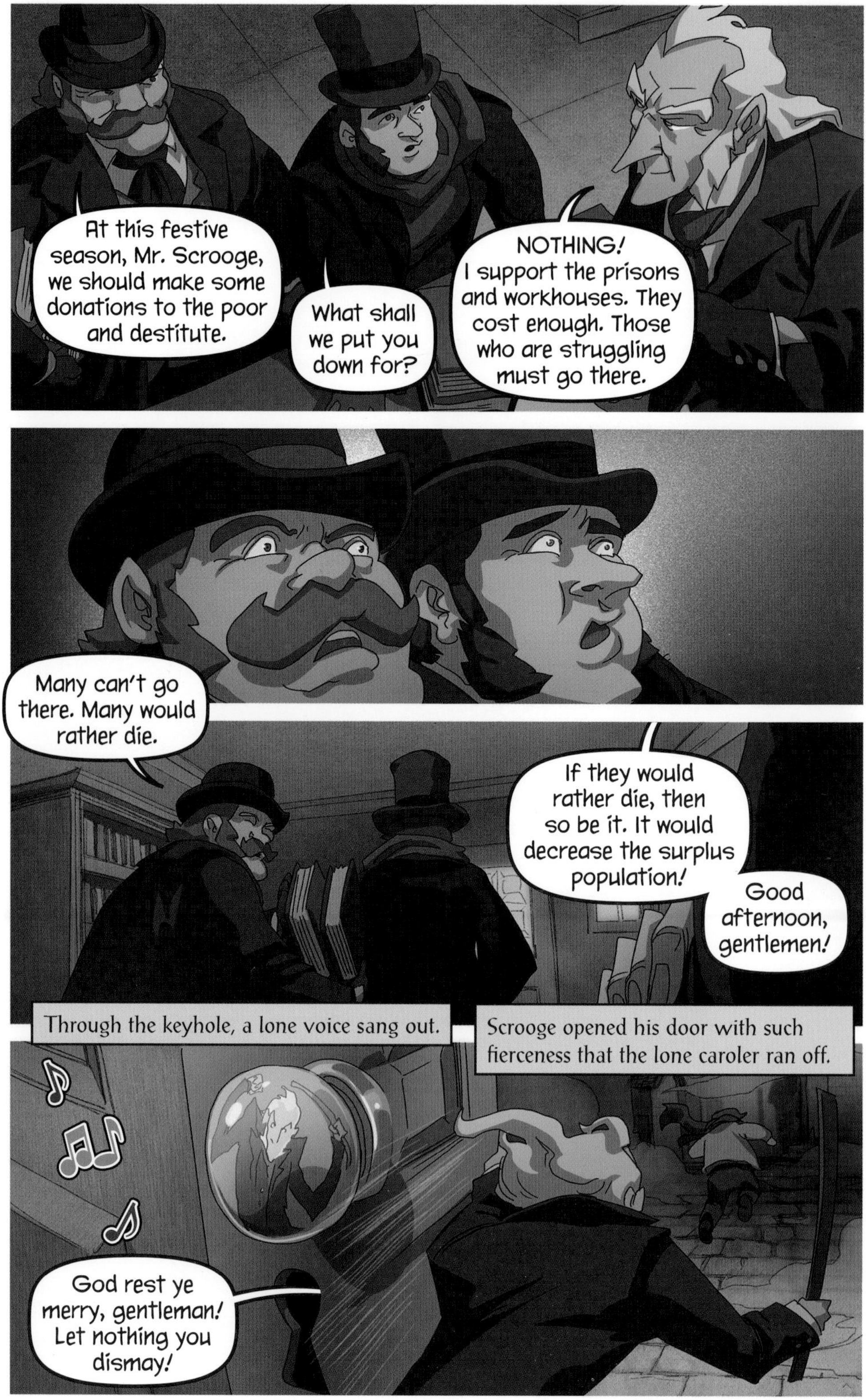
At this festive season, Mr. Scrooge, we should make some donations to the poor and destitute.
What shall we put you down for?
NOTHING! I support the prisons and workhouses. They cost enough. Those who are struggling must go there.
Many can't go there. Many would rather die.
If they would rather die, then so be it. It would decrease the surplus population!
Good afternoon, gentlemen!
Through the keyhole, a lone voice sang out.
Scrooge opened his door with such fierceness that the lone caroler ran off.
God rest ye merry, gentleman! Let nothing you dismay!

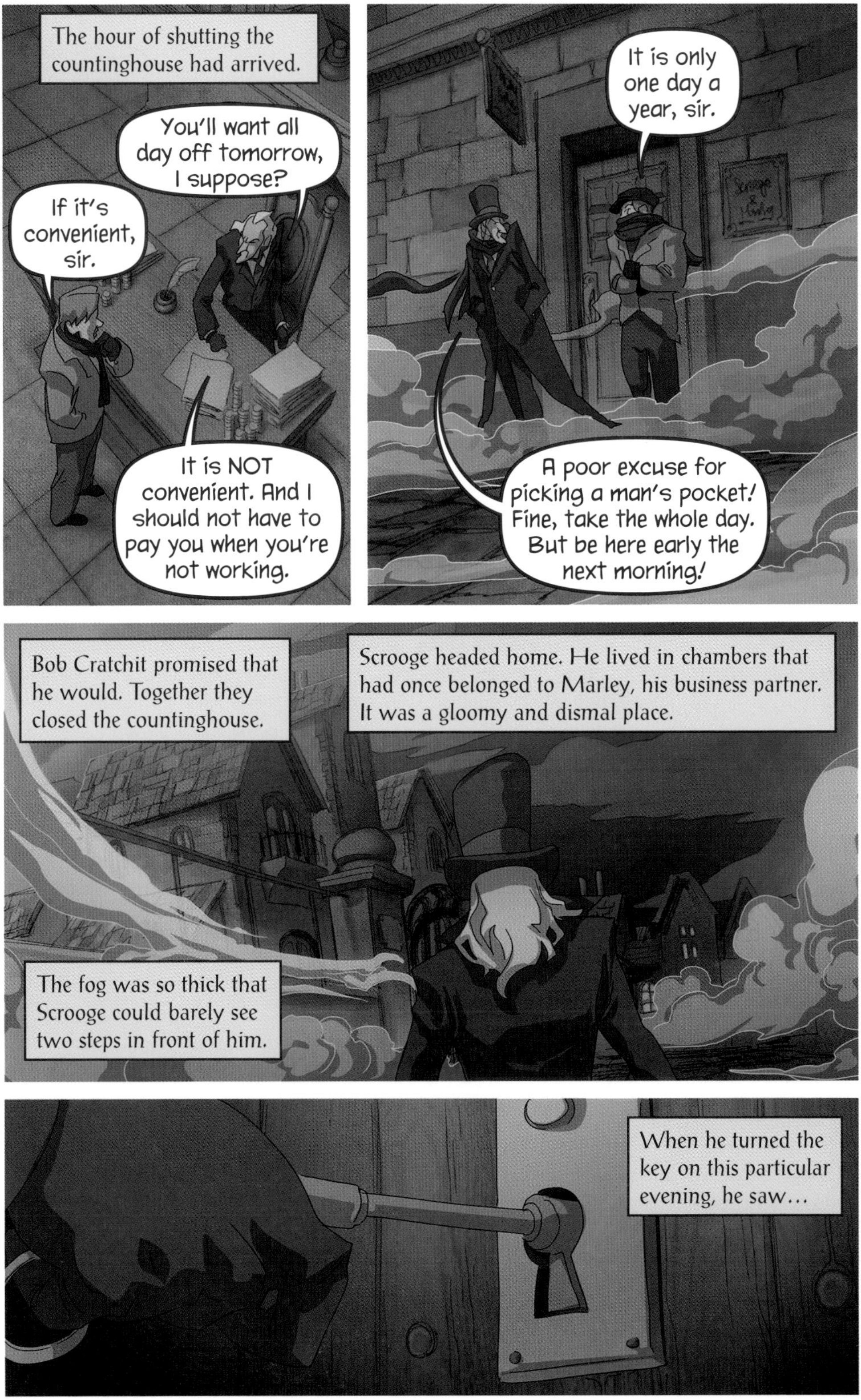
The hour of shutting the countinghouse had arrived.
You'll want all day off tomorrow, I suppose?
If it's convenient, sir.
It is NOT convenient. And I should not have to pay you when you're not working.
It is only one day a year, sir.
A poor excuse for picking a man's pocket! Fine, take the whole day. But be here early the next morning!
Bob Cratchit promised that he would. Together they closed the countinghouse.
Scrooge headed home. He lived in chambers that had once belonged to Marley, his business partner. It was a gloomy and dismal place.
The fog was so thick that Scrooge could barely see two steps in front of him.
When he turned the key on this particular evening, he saw…

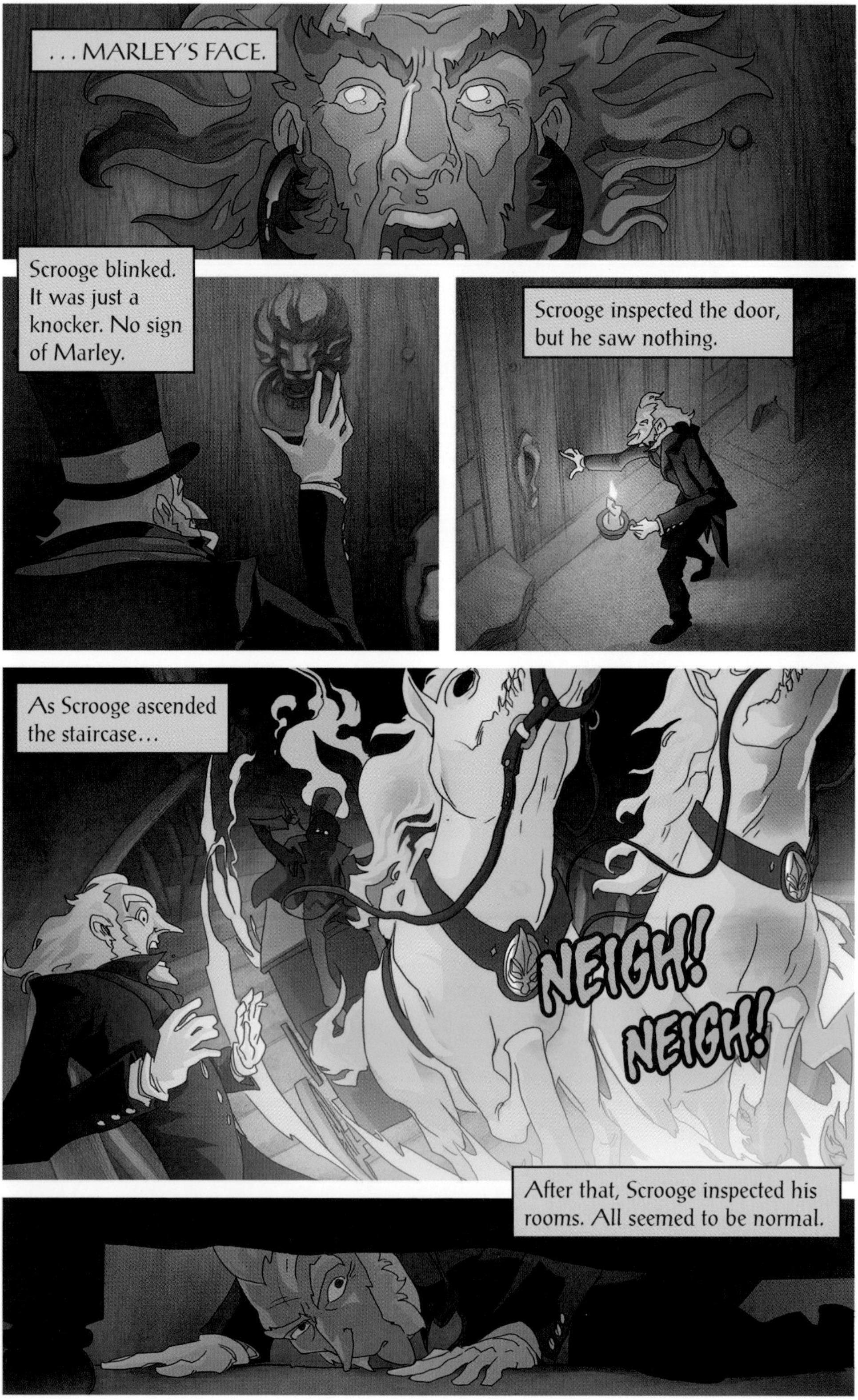

. . . MARLEY'S FACE.
Scrooge blinked. It was just a knocker. No sign of Marley.
Scrooge inspected the door, but he saw nothing.
As Scrooge ascended the staircase...
NEIGH!
NEIGH!
After that, Scrooge inspected his rooms. All seemed to be normal.

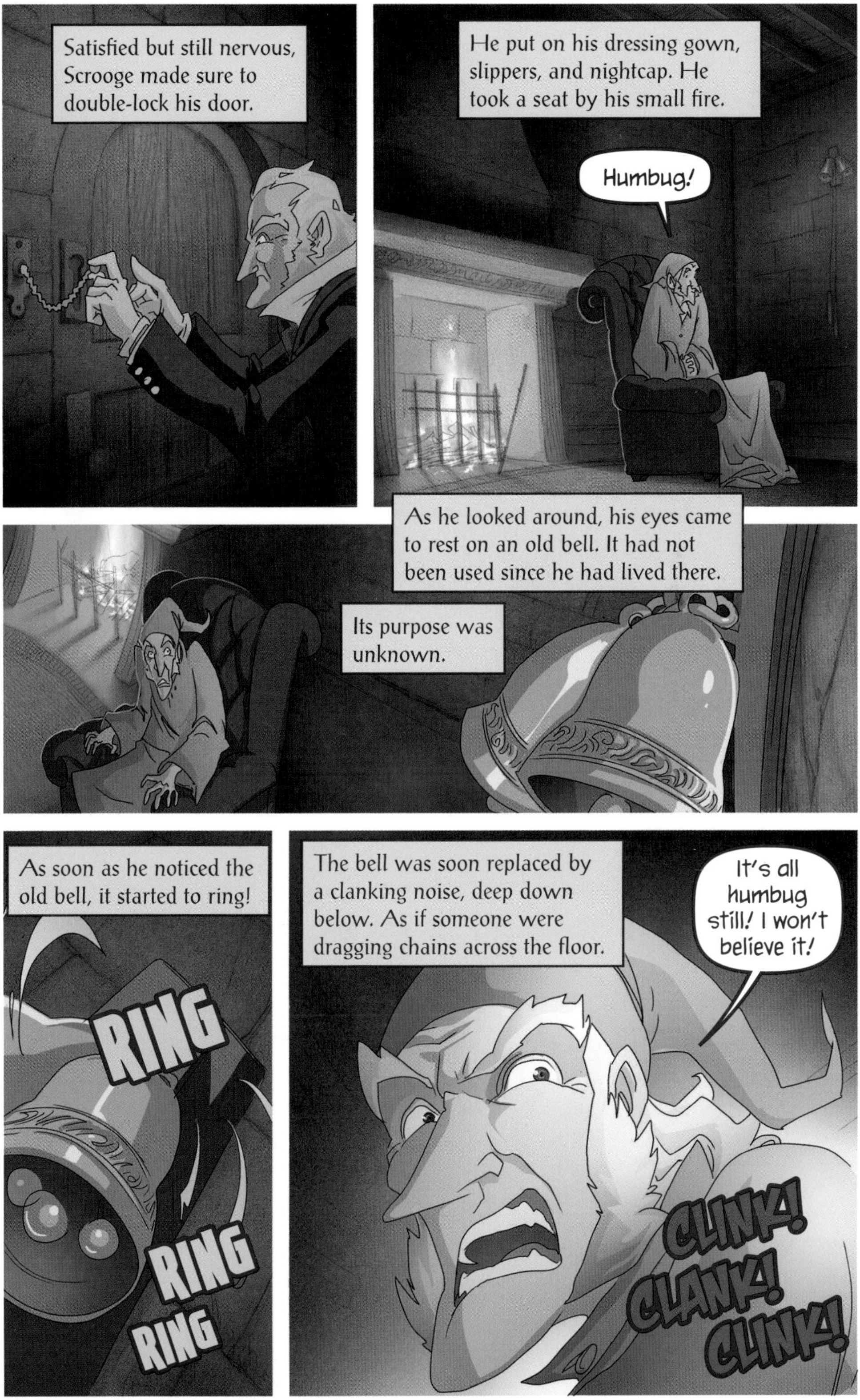
Satisfied but still nervous, Scrooge made sure to double-lock his door.
He put on his dressing gown, slippers, and nightcap. He took a seat by his small fire.
Humbug!
As he looked around, his eyes came to rest on an old bell. It had not been used since he had lived there.
Its purpose was unknown.
As soon as he noticed the old bell, it started to ring!
RING
RING
RING
The bell was soon replaced by a clanking noise, deep down below. As if someone were dragging chains across the floor.
It's all humbug still! I won't believe it!
CLINK!
CLANK!
CLINK!

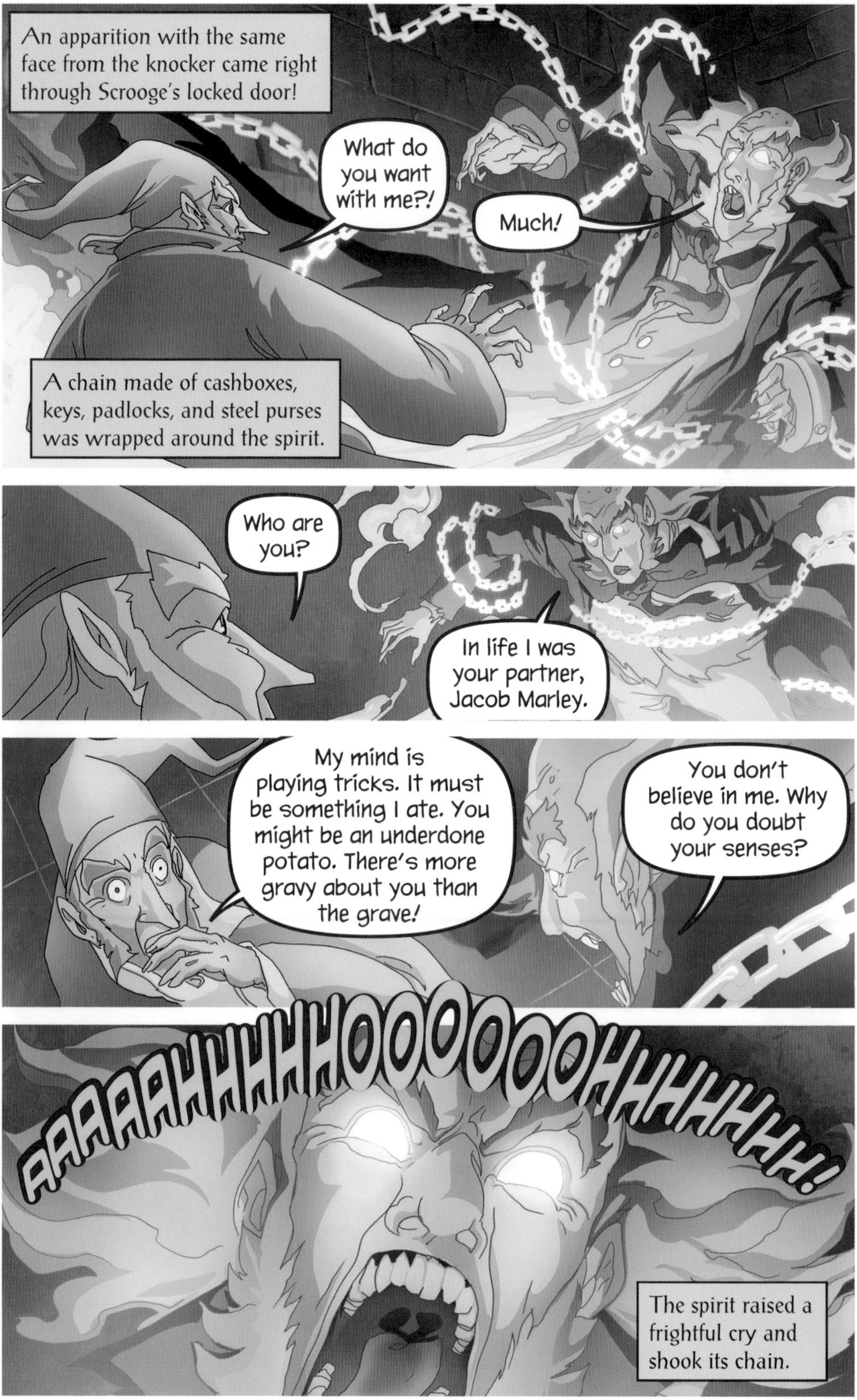

An apparition with the same face from the knocker came right through Scrooge's locked door!
What do you want with me?!
Much!
A chain made of cashboxes, keys, padlocks, and steel purses was wrapped around the spirit.
Who are you?
In life I was your partner, Jacob Marley.
My mind is playing tricks. It must be something I ate. You might be an underdone potato. There's more gravy about you than the grave!
You don't believe in me. Why do you doubt your senses?
AAAAAHHHHHOOOOOOOHHHHHHH!
The spirit raised a frightful cry and shook its chain.

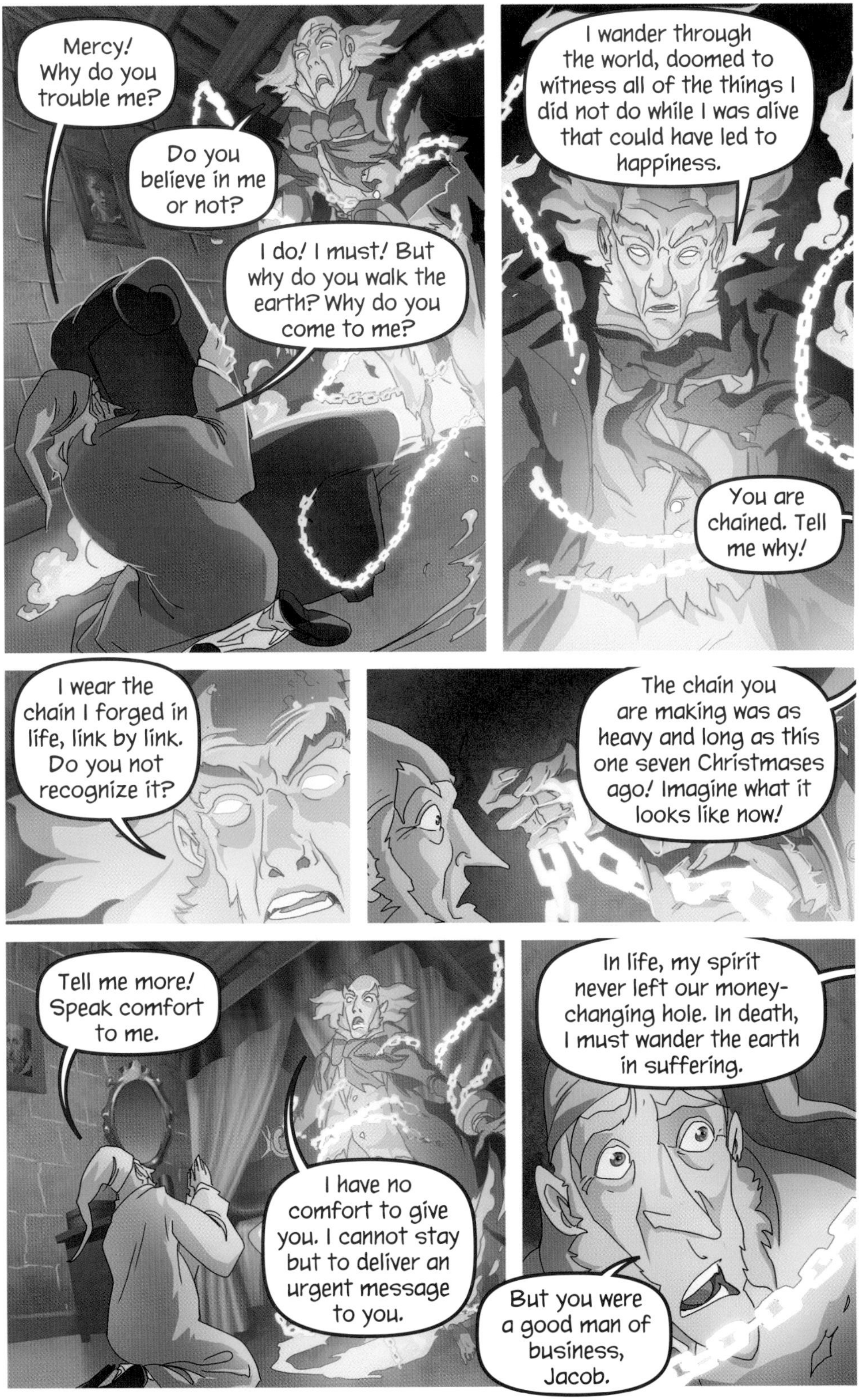

Mercy! Why do you trouble me?
Do you believe in me or not?
I do! I must! But why do you walk the earth? Why do you come to me?
I wander through the world, doomed to witness all of the things I did not do while I was alive that could have led to happiness.
You are chained. Tell me why!
I wear the chain I forged in life, link by link. Do you not recognize it?
The chain you are making was as heavy and long as this one seven Christmases ago! Imagine what it looks like now!
Tell me more! Speak comfort to me.
I have no comfort to give you. I cannot stay but to deliver an urgent message to you.
In life, my spirit never left our money-changing hole. In death, I must wander the earth in suffering.
But you were a good man of business, Jacob.

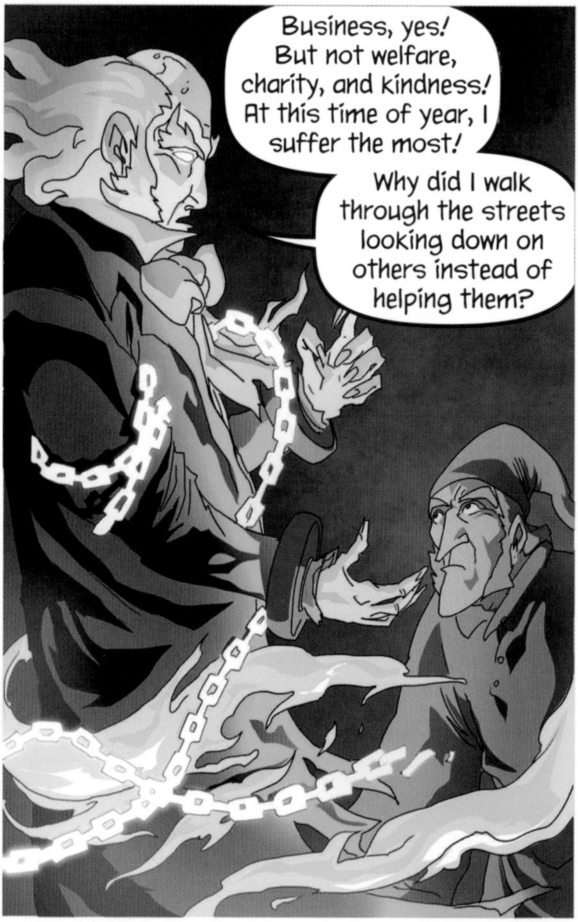
Business, yes! But not welfare, charity, and kindness! At this time of year, I suffer the most!
Why did I walk through the streets looking down on others instead of helping them?

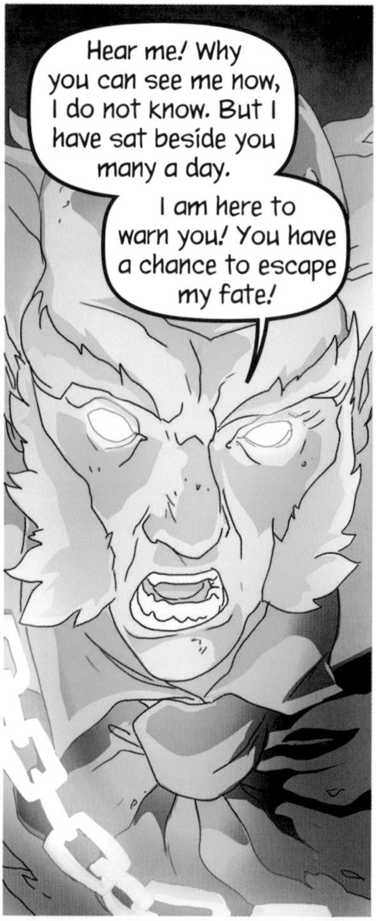
Hear me! Why you can see me now, I do not know. But I have sat beside you many a day.
I am here to warn you! You have a chance to escape my fate!

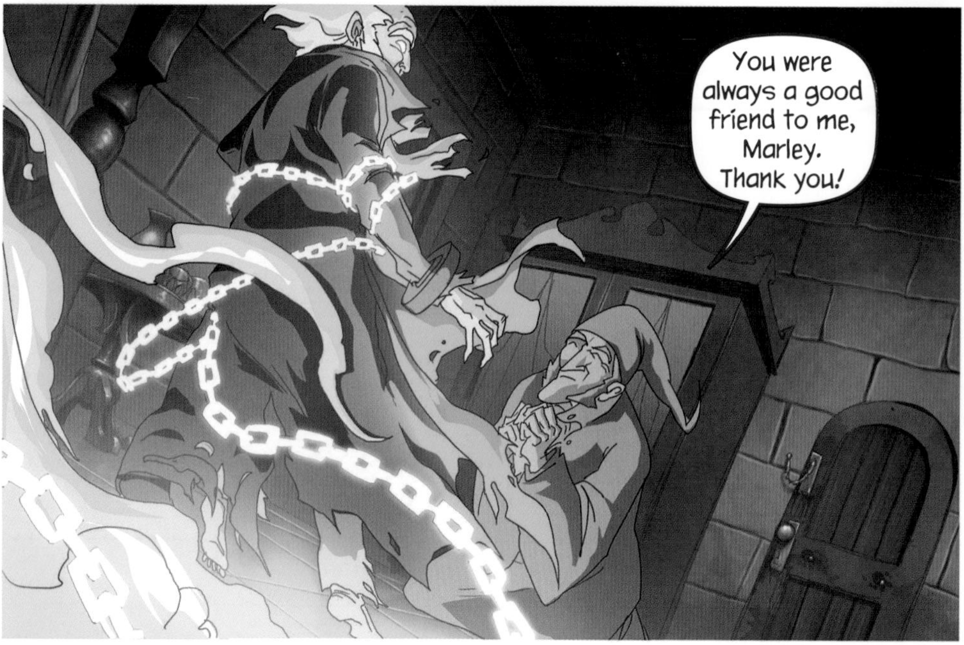
You were always a good friend to me, Marley. Thank you!

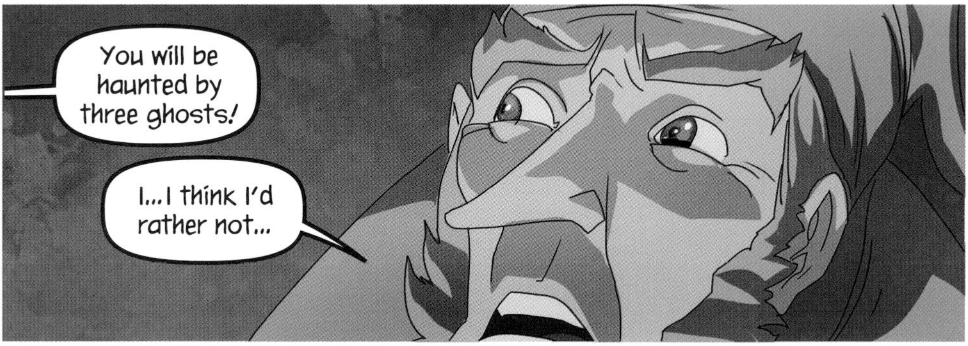
You will be haunted by three ghosts!
I...I think I'd rather not...

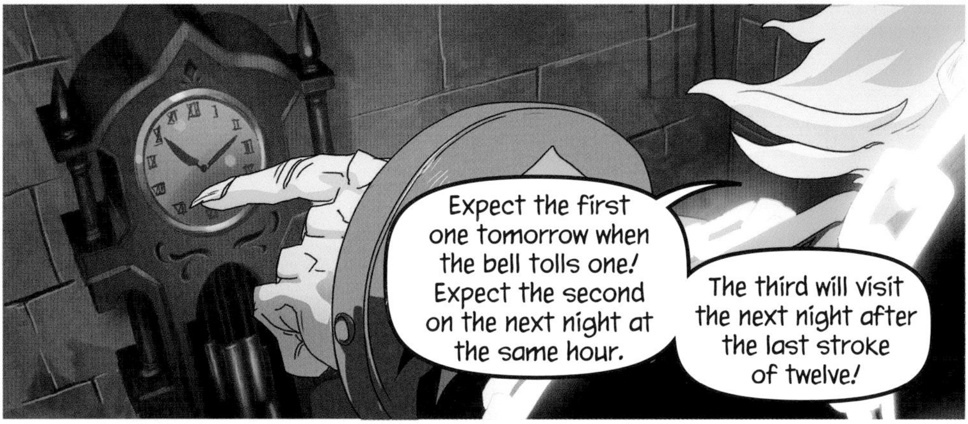
Expect the first one tomorrow when the bell tolls one! Expect the second on the next night at the same hour.
The third will visit the next night after the last stroke of twelve!

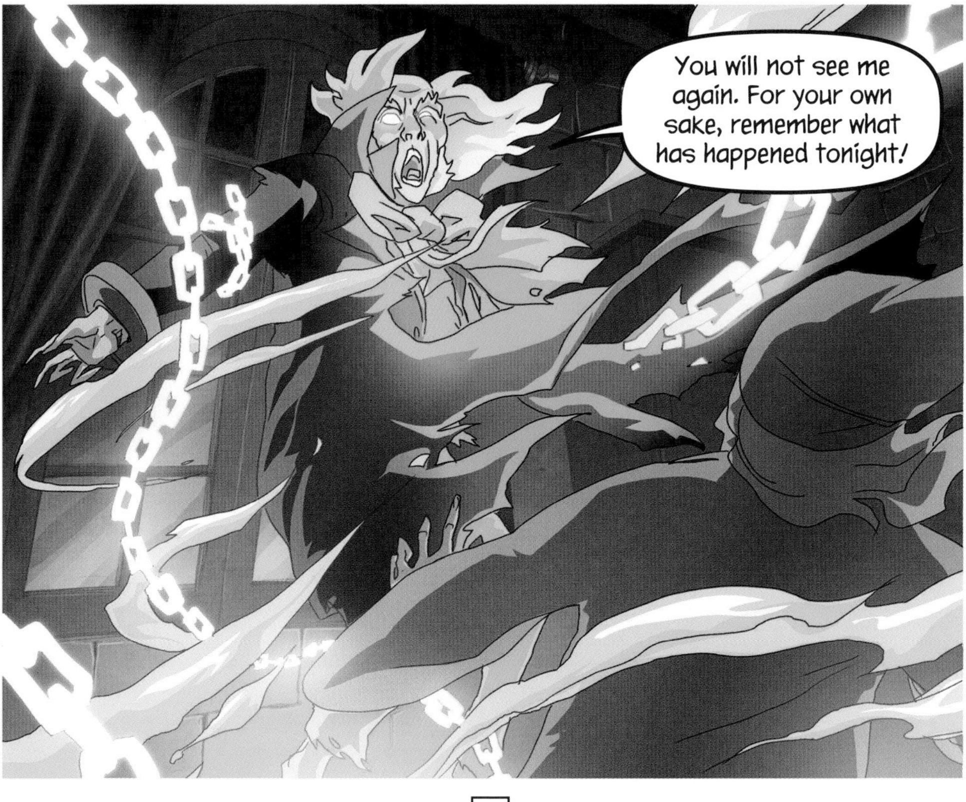
You will not see me again. For your own sake, remember what has happened tonight!

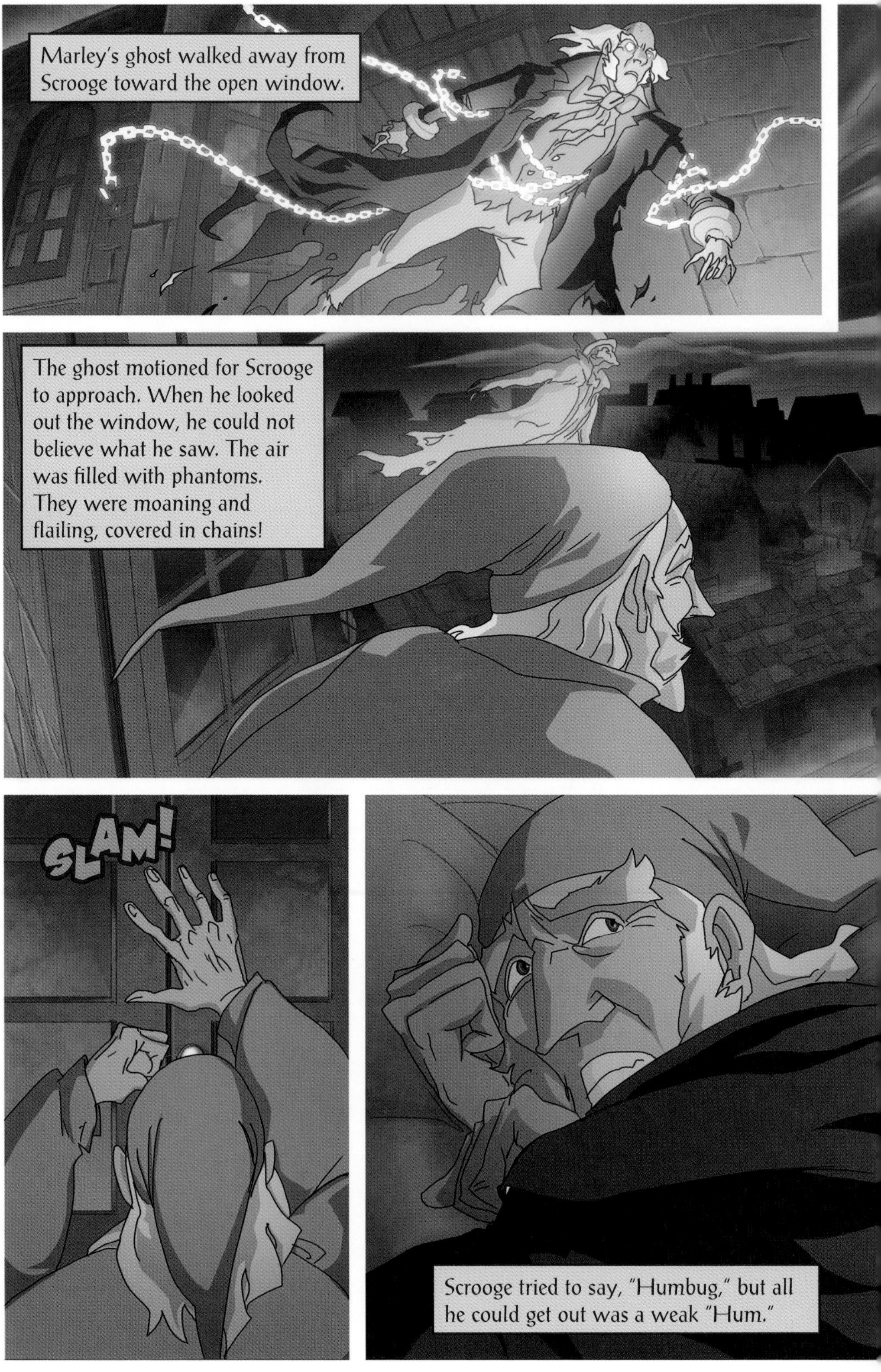
Marley's ghost walked away from Scrooge toward the open window.
The ghost motioned for Scrooge to approach. When he looked out the window, he could not believe what he saw. The air was filled with phantoms. They were moaning and flailing, covered in chains!
SLAM!
Scrooge tried to say, "Humbug," but all he could get out was a weak "Hum."

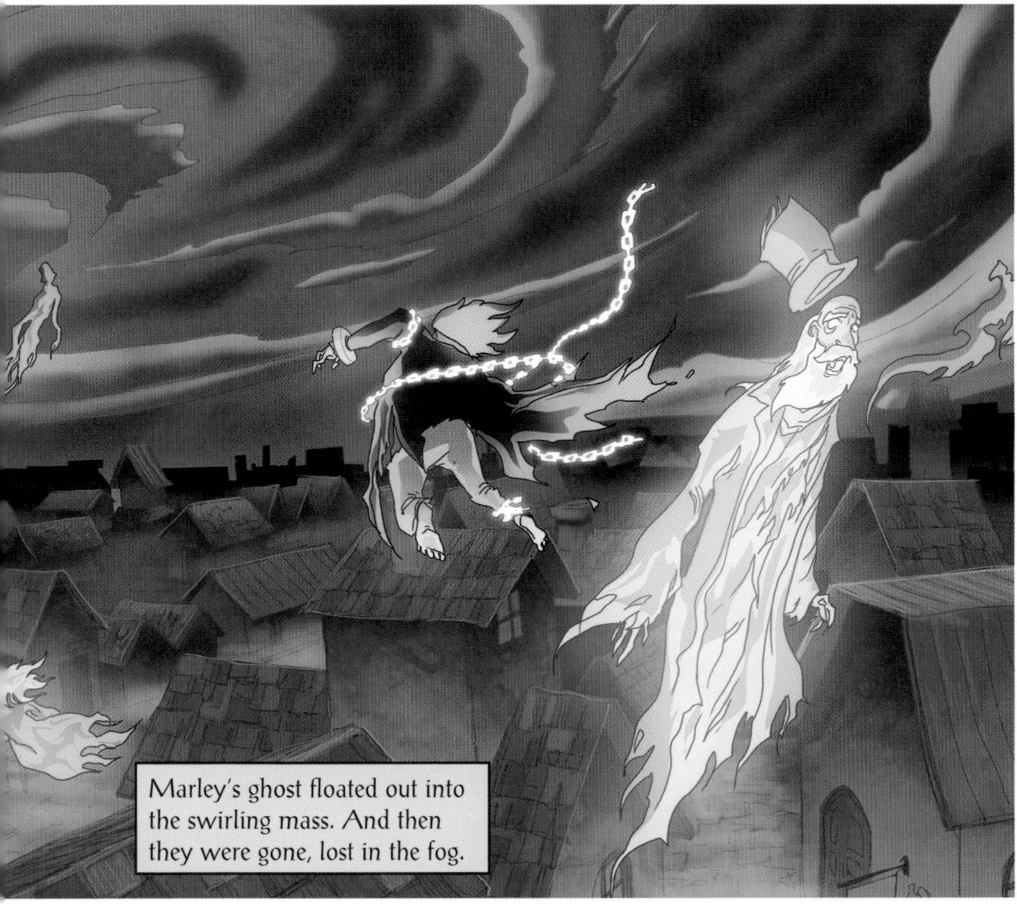
Marley's ghost floated out into the swirling mass. And then they were gone, lost in the fog.

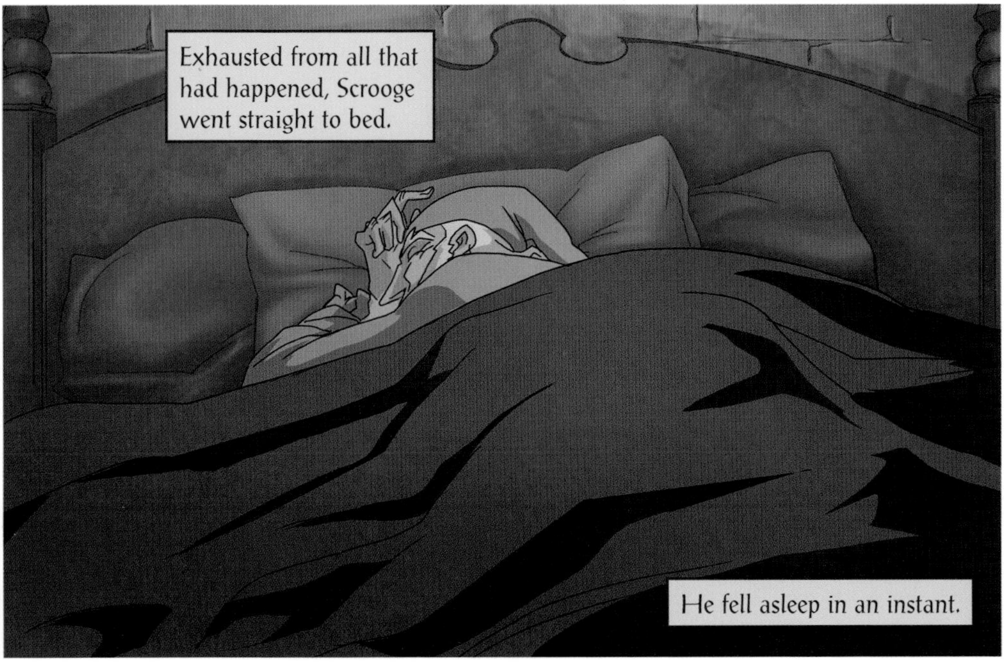
Exhausted from all that had happened, Scrooge went straight to bed.
He fell asleep in an instant.

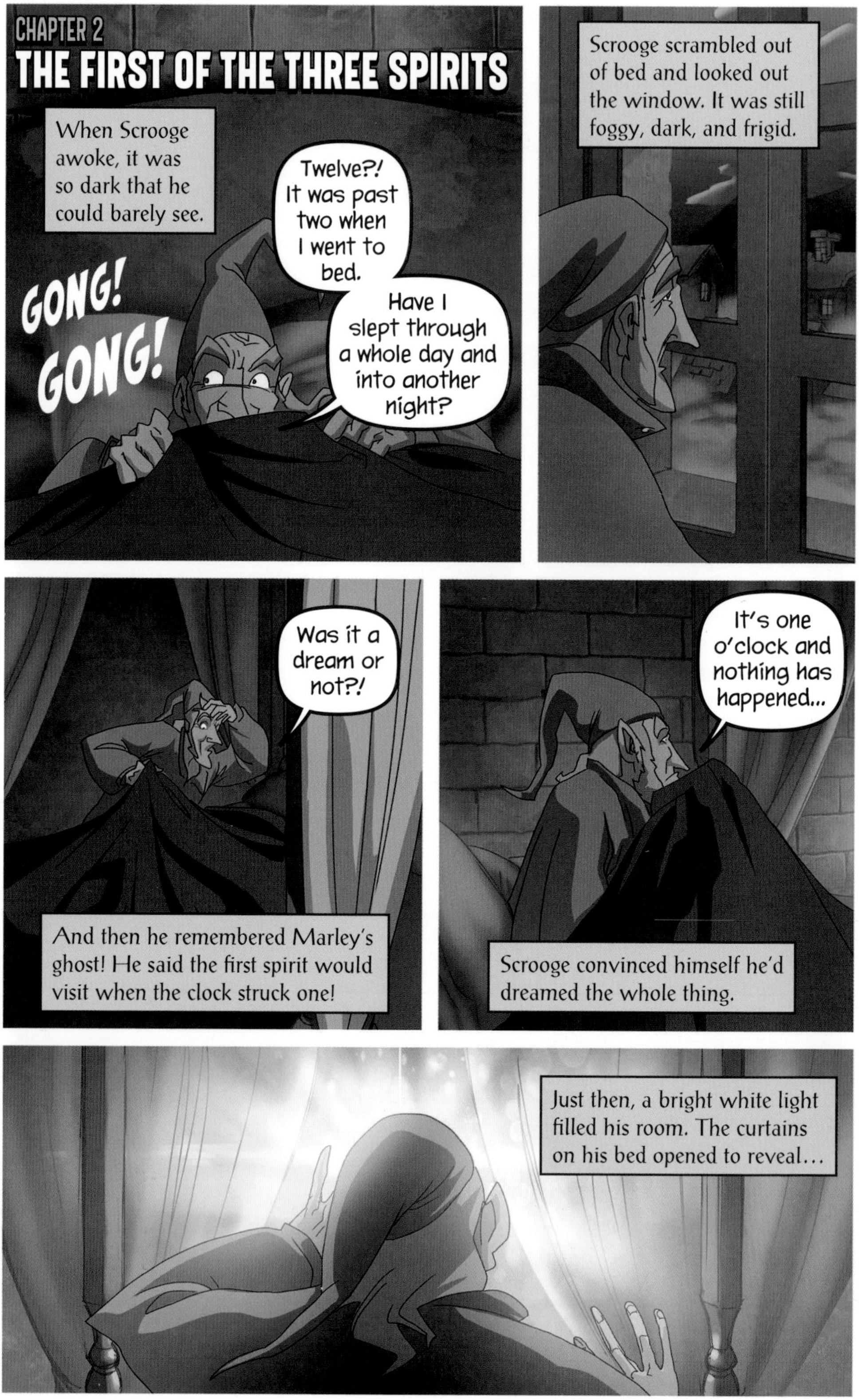
CHAPTER 2
THE FIRST OF THE THREE SPIRITS
When Scrooge awoke, it was so dark that he could barely see.
GONG!
GONG!
Twelve?! It was past two when I went to bed.
Have I slept through a whole day and into another night?
Scrooge scrambled out of bed and looked out the window. It was still foggy, dark, and frigid.
Was it a dream or not?!
And then he remembered Marley's ghost! He said the first spirit would visit when the clock struck one!
It's one o'clock and nothing has happened...
Scrooge convinced himself he'd dreamed the whole thing.
Just then, a bright white light filled his room. The curtains on his bed opened to reveal...

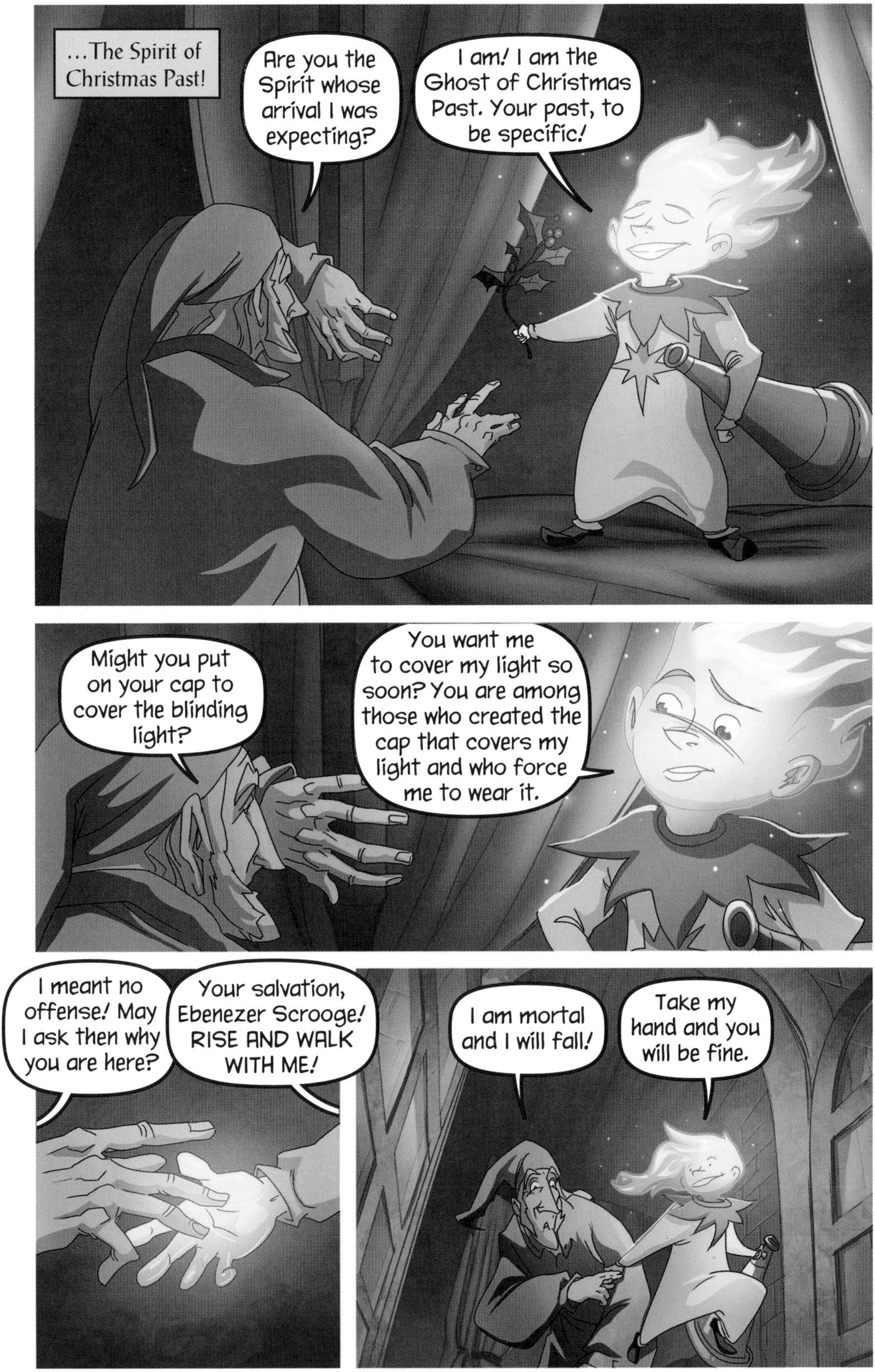
...The Spirit of Christmas Past!
Are you the Spirit whose arrival I was expecting?
I am! I am the Ghost of Christmas Past. Your past, to be specific!
Might you put on your cap to cover the blinding light?
You want me to cover my light so soon? You are among those who created the cap that covers my light and who force me to wear it.
I meant no offense! May I ask then why you are here?
Your salvation, Ebenezer Scrooge! RISE AND WALK WITH ME!
I am mortal and I will fall!
Take my hand and you will be fine.

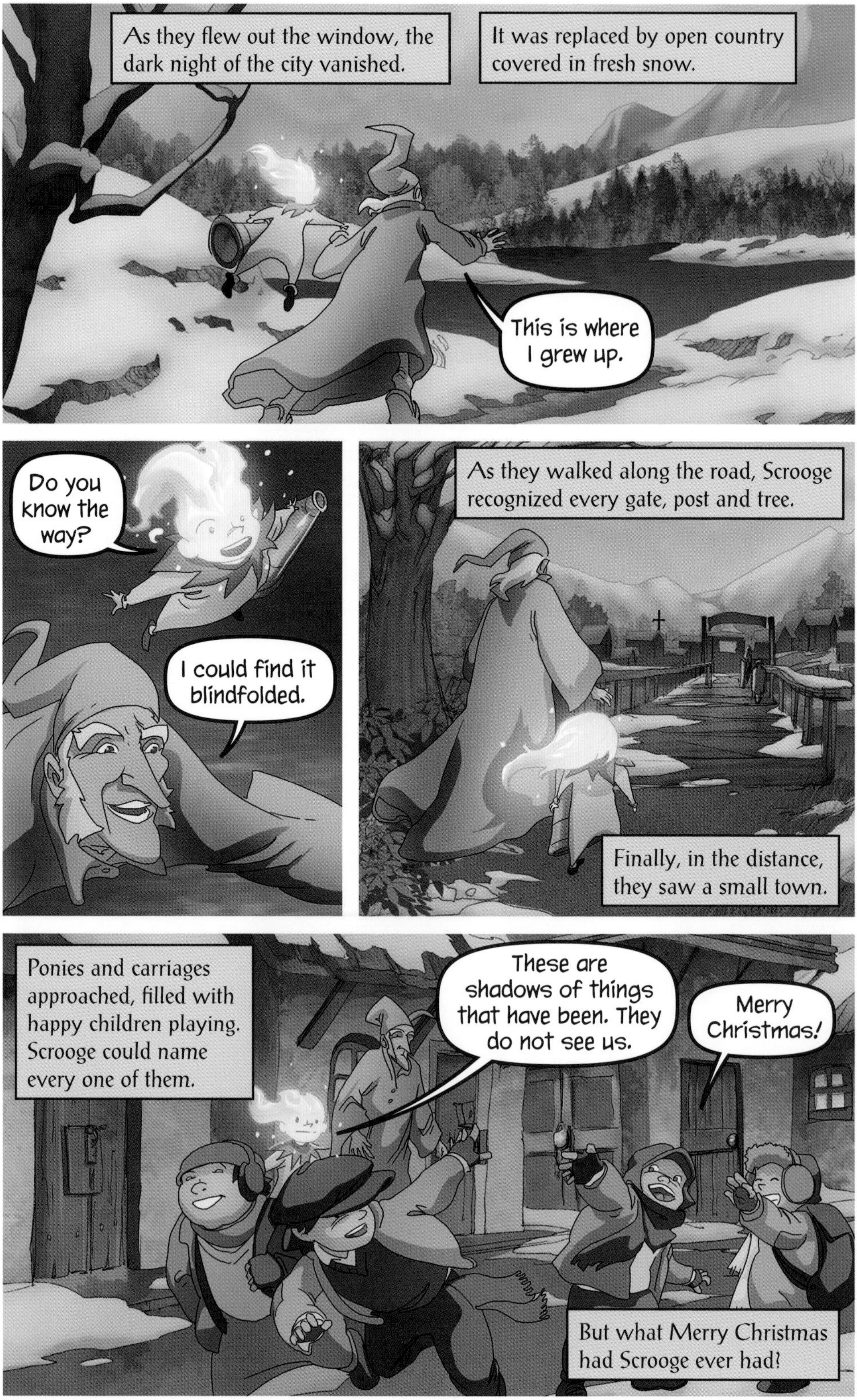

As they flew out the window, the dark night of the city vanished.
It was replaced by open country covered in fresh snow.
This is where I grew up.
Do you know the way?
I could find it blindfolded.
As they walked along the road, Scrooge recognized every gate, post and tree.
Finally, in the distance, they saw a small town.
Ponies and carriages approached, filled with happy children playing. Scrooge could name every one of them.
These are shadows of things that have been. They do not see us.
Merry Christmas!
But what Merry Christmas had Scrooge ever had?

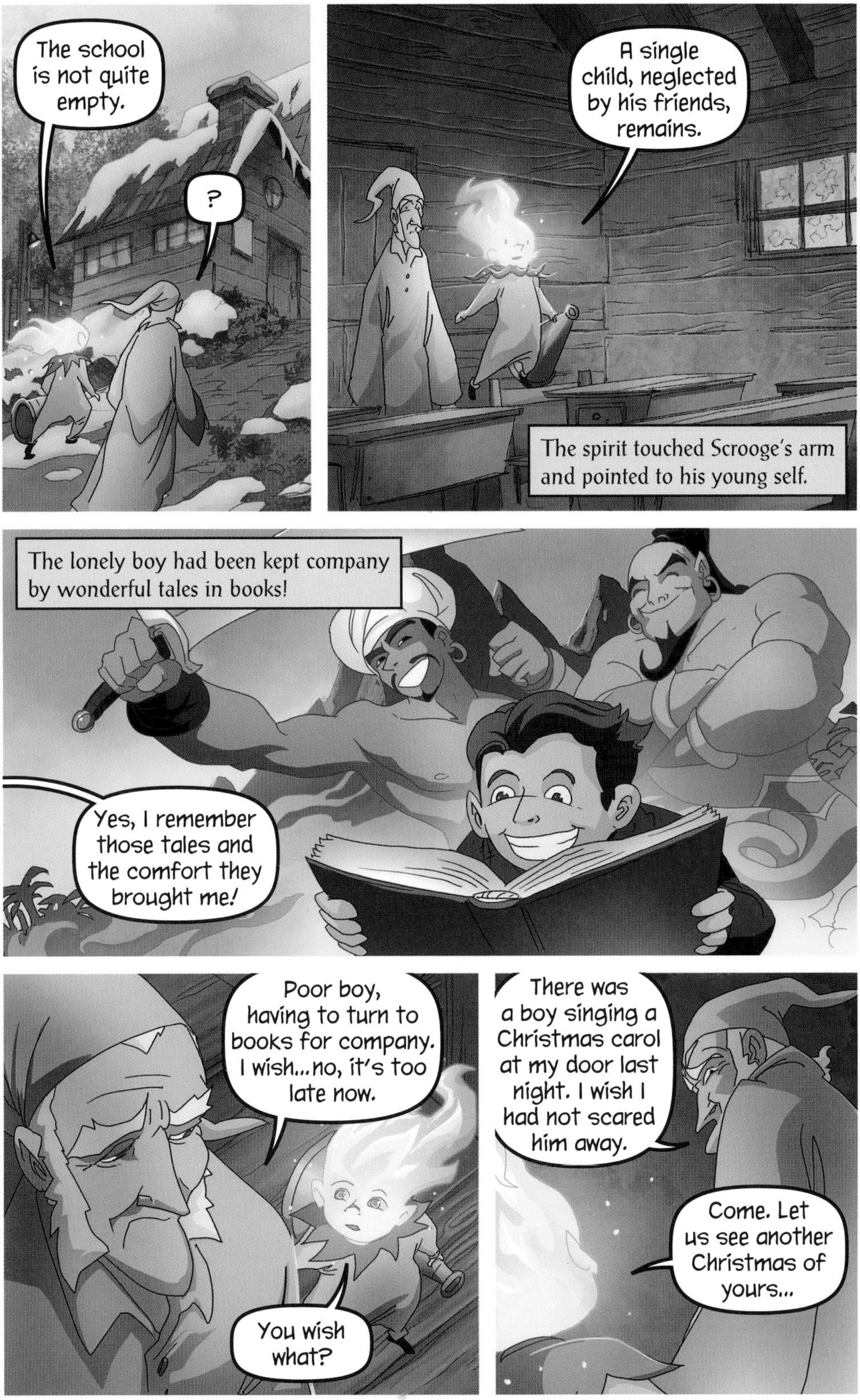
The school is not quite empty.
?
A single child, neglected by his friends, remains.
The spirit touched Scrooge's arm and pointed to his young self.
The lonely boy had been kept company by wonderful tales in books!
Yes, I remember those tales and the comfort they brought me!
Poor boy, having to turn to books for company. I wish...no, it's too late now.
You wish what?
There was a boy singing a Christmas carol at my door last night. I wish I had not scared him away.
Come. Let us see another Christmas of yours...

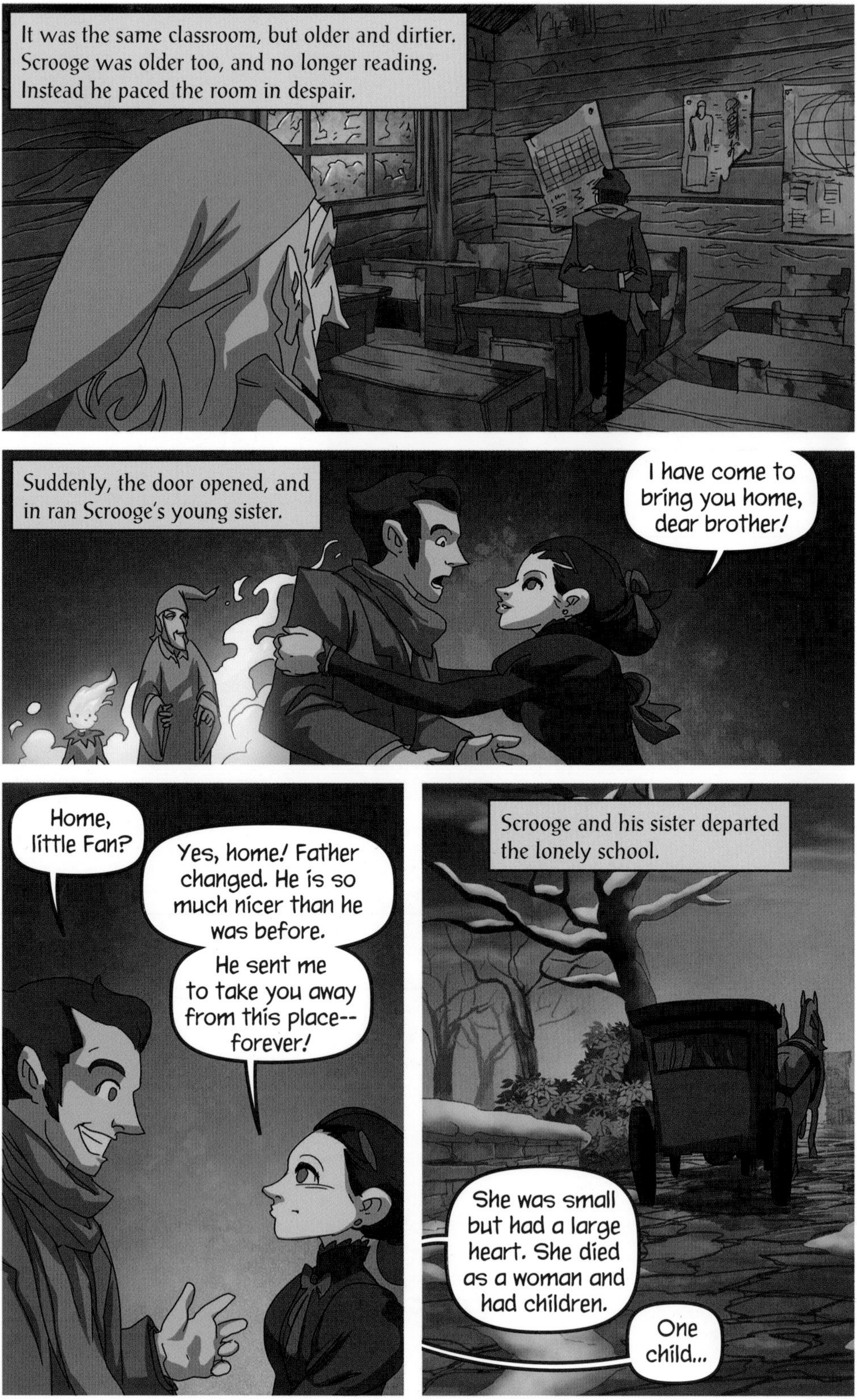
It was the same classroom, but older and dirtier. Scrooge was older too, and no longer reading. Instead he paced the room in despair.
Suddenly, the door opened, and in ran Scrooge's young sister.
I have come to bring you home, dear brother!
Home, little Fan?
Yes, home! Father changed. He is so much nicer than he was before.
He sent me to take you away from this place-- forever!
Scrooge and his sister departed the lonely school.
She was small but had a large heart. She died as a woman and had children.
One child...

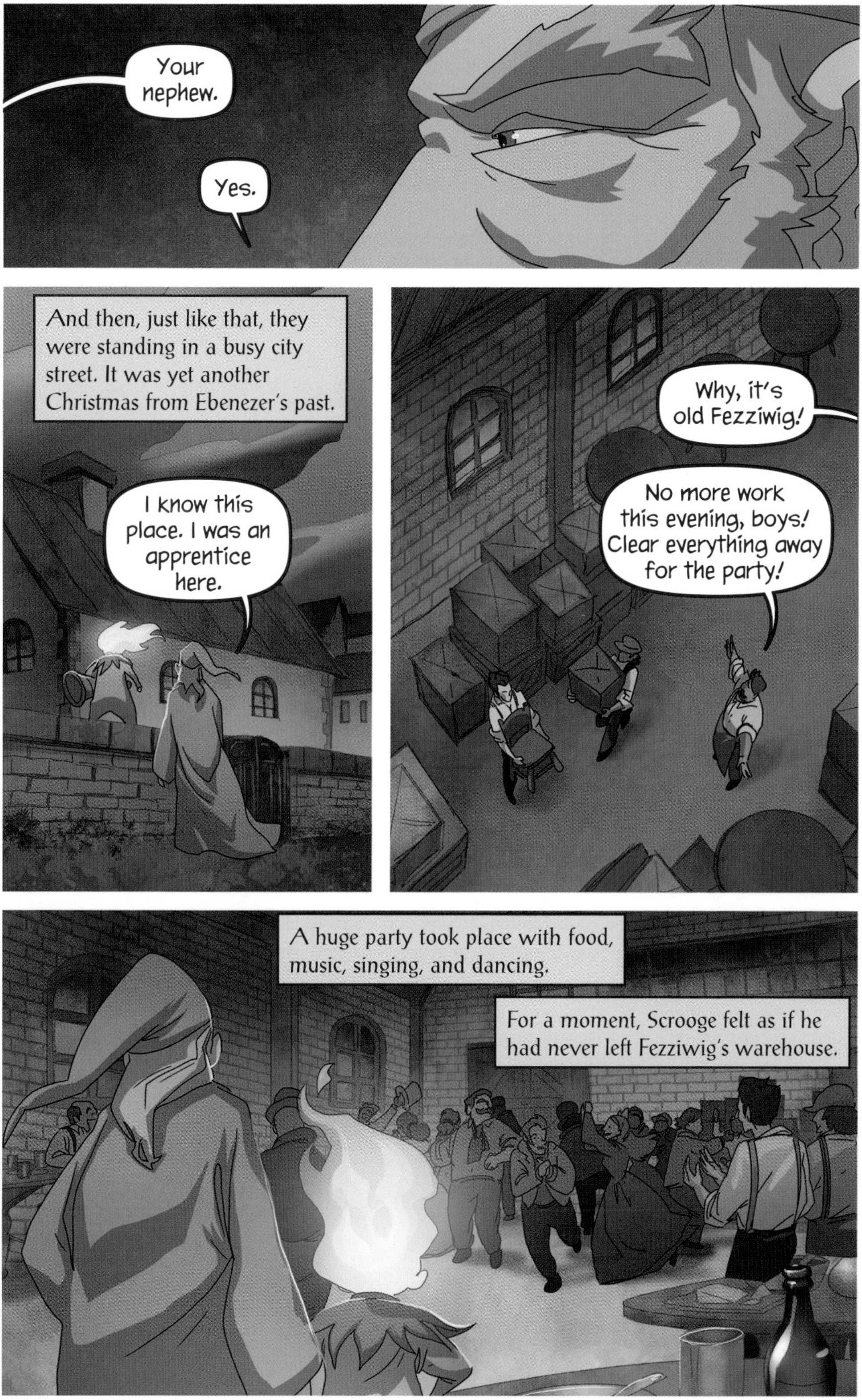
Your nephew.
Yes.
And then, just like that, they were standing in a busy city street. It was yet another Christmas from Ebenezer's past.
I know this place. I was an apprentice here.
Why, it's old Fezziwig!
No more work this evening, boys! Clear everything away for the party!
A huge party took place with food, music, singing, and dancing.
For a moment, Scrooge felt as if he had never left Fezziwig's warehouse.

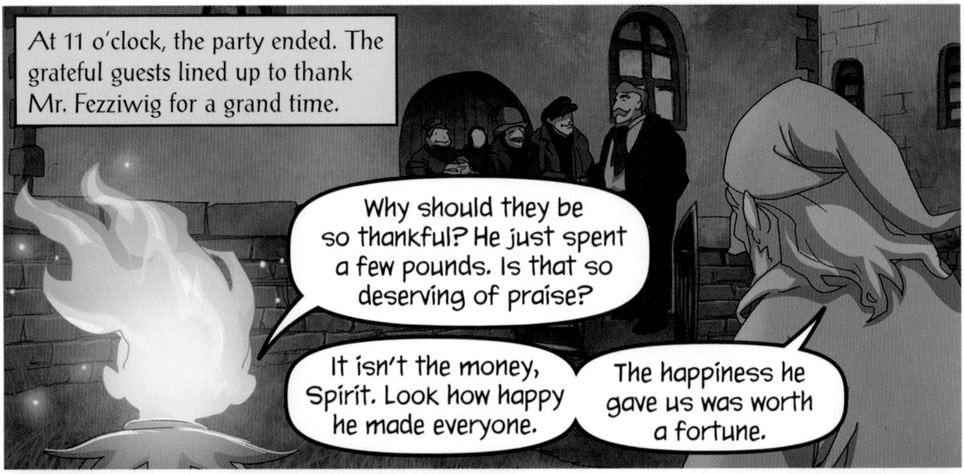
At 11 o'clock, the party ended. The grateful guests lined up to thank Mr. Fezziwig for a grand time.
Why should they be so thankful? He just spent a few pounds. Is that so deserving of praise?
It isn't the money, Spirit. Look how happy he made everyone.
The happiness he gave us was worth a fortune.

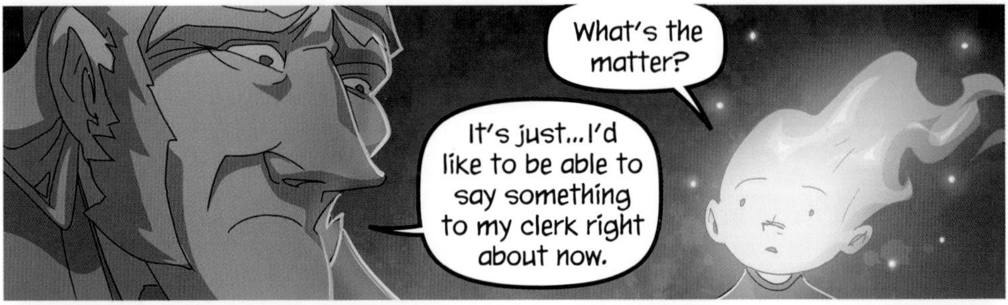
What's the matter?
It's just...I'd like to be able to say something to my clerk right about now.

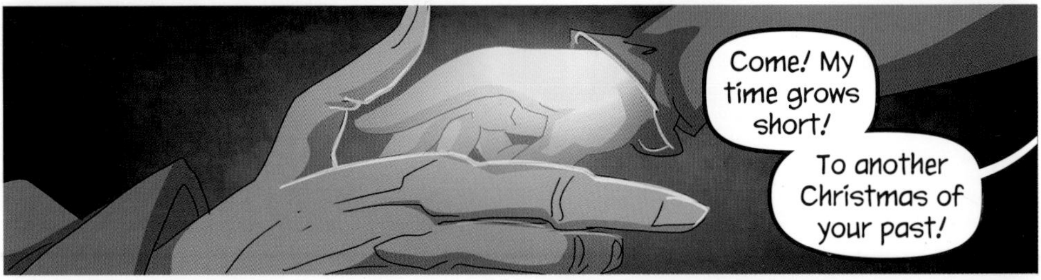
Come! My time grows short!
To another Christmas of your past!

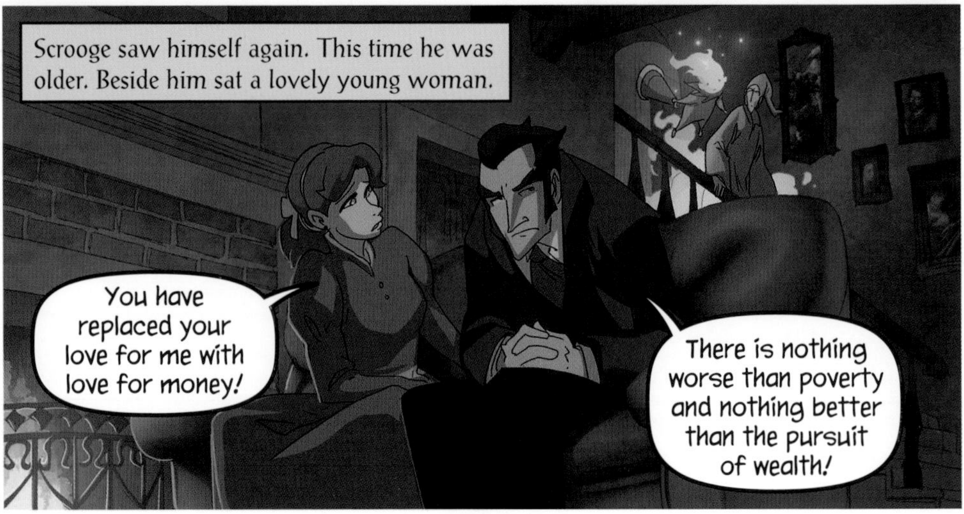
Scrooge saw himself again. This time he was older. Beside him sat a lovely young woman.
You have replaced your love for me with love for money!
There is nothing worse than poverty and nothing better than the pursuit of wealth!

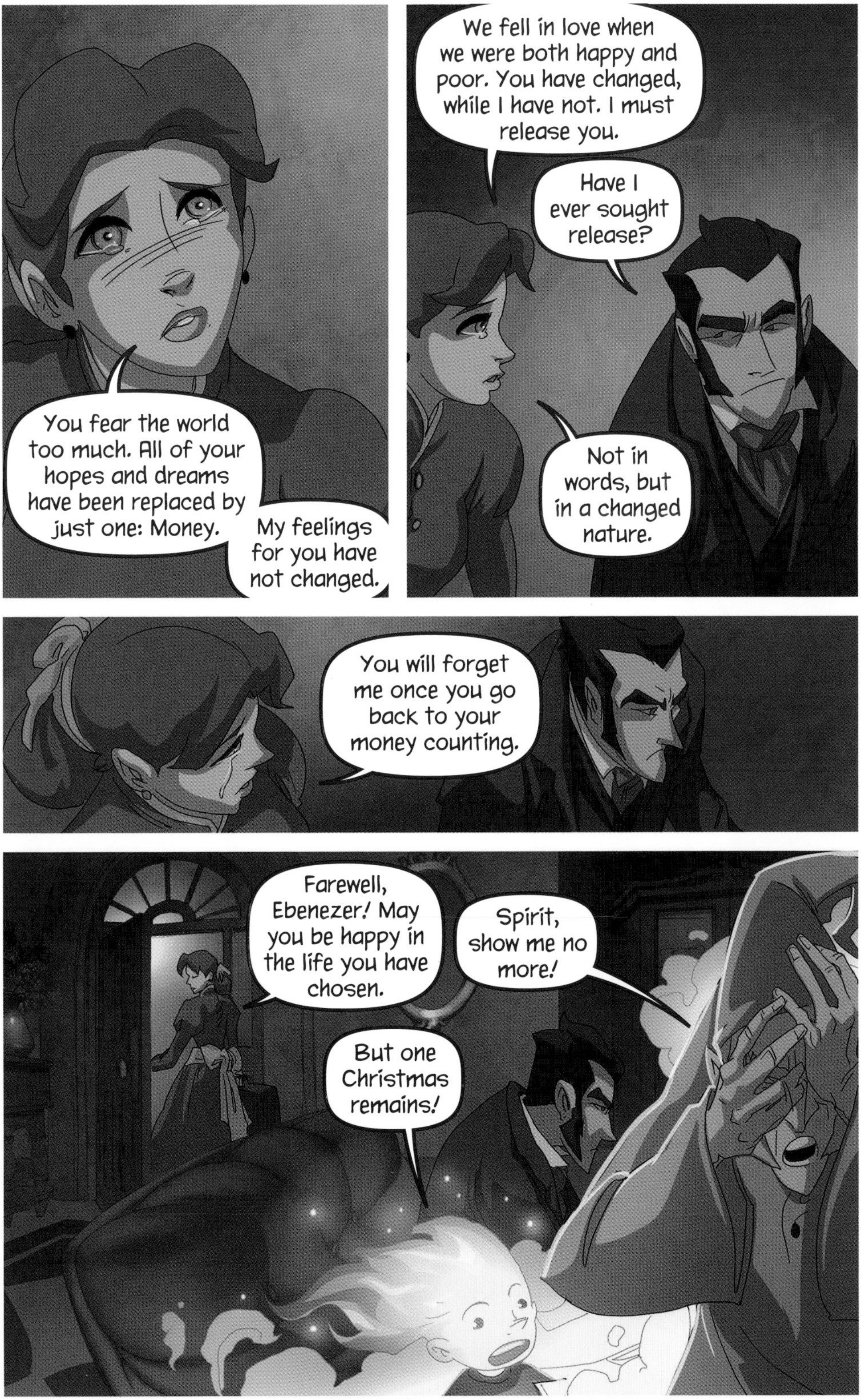
You fear the world too much. All of your hopes and dreams have been replaced by just one: Money.
My feelings for you have not changed.
We fell in love when we were both happy and poor. You have changed, while I have not. I must release you.
Have I ever sought release?
Not in words, but in a changed nature.
You will forget me once you go back to your money counting.
Farewell, Ebenezer! May you be happy in the life you have chosen.
Spirit, show me no more!
But one Christmas remains!

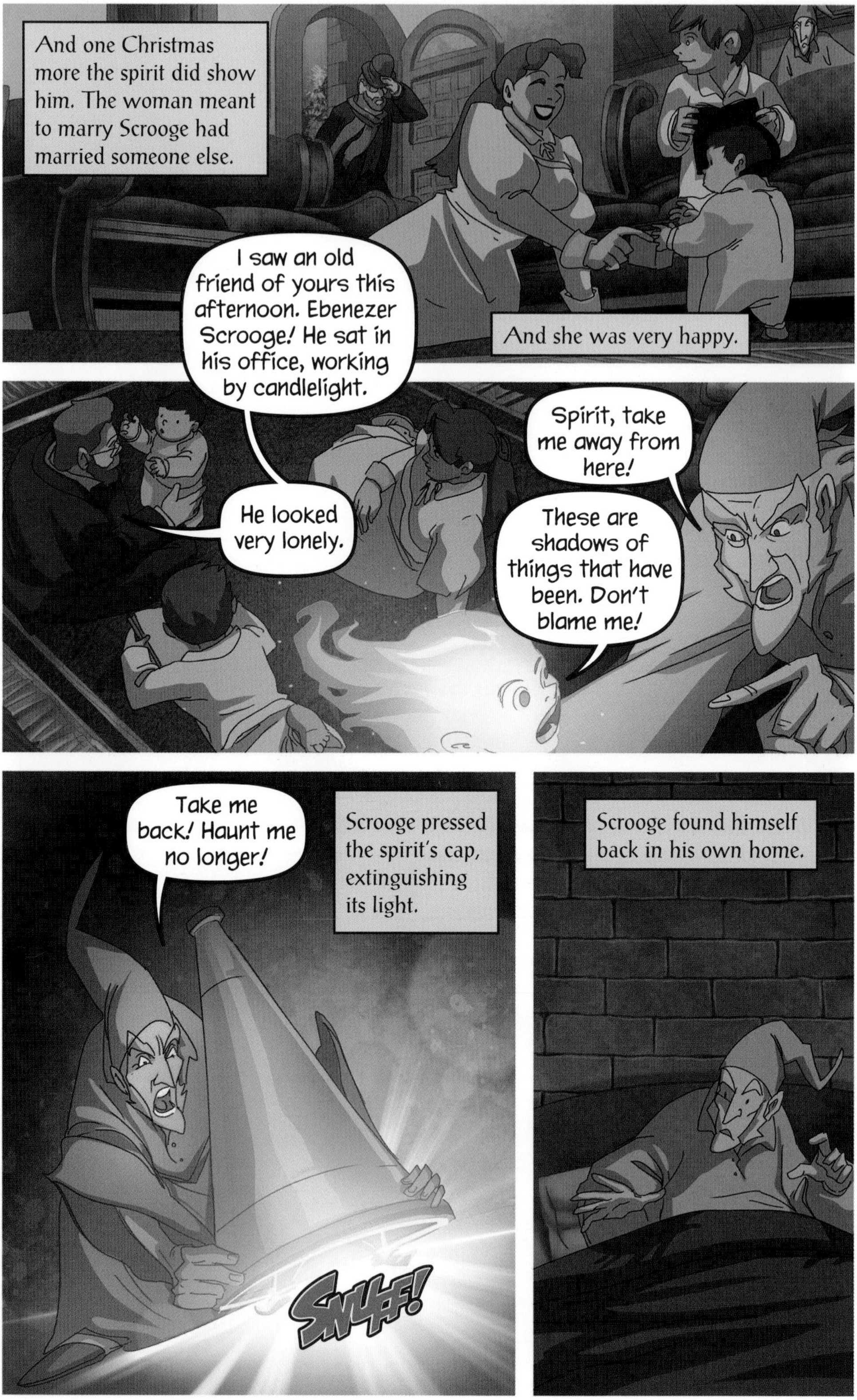
And one Christmas more the spirit did show him. The woman meant to marry Scrooge had married someone else.
I saw an old friend of yours this afternoon. Ebenezer Scrooge! He sat in his office, working by candlelight.
And she was very happy.
He looked very lonely.
Spirit, take me away from here!
These are shadows of things that have been. Don't blame me!
Take me back! Haunt me no longer!
Scrooge pressed the spirit's cap, extinguishing its light.
SNUFF!
Scrooge found himself back in his own home.

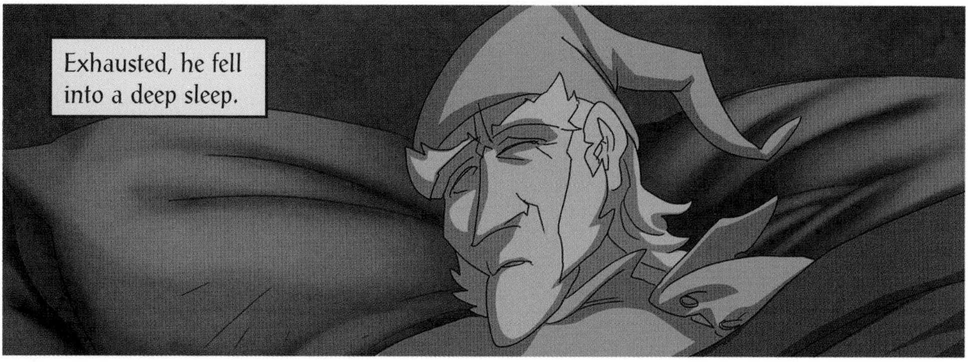
Exhausted, he fell into a deep sleep.

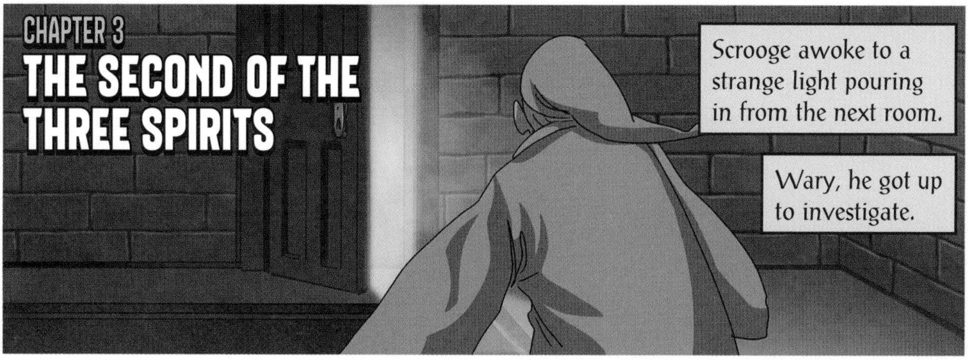
CHAPTER 3
THE SECOND OF THE THREE SPIRITS
Scrooge awoke to a strange light pouring in from the next room.
Wary, he got up to investigate.

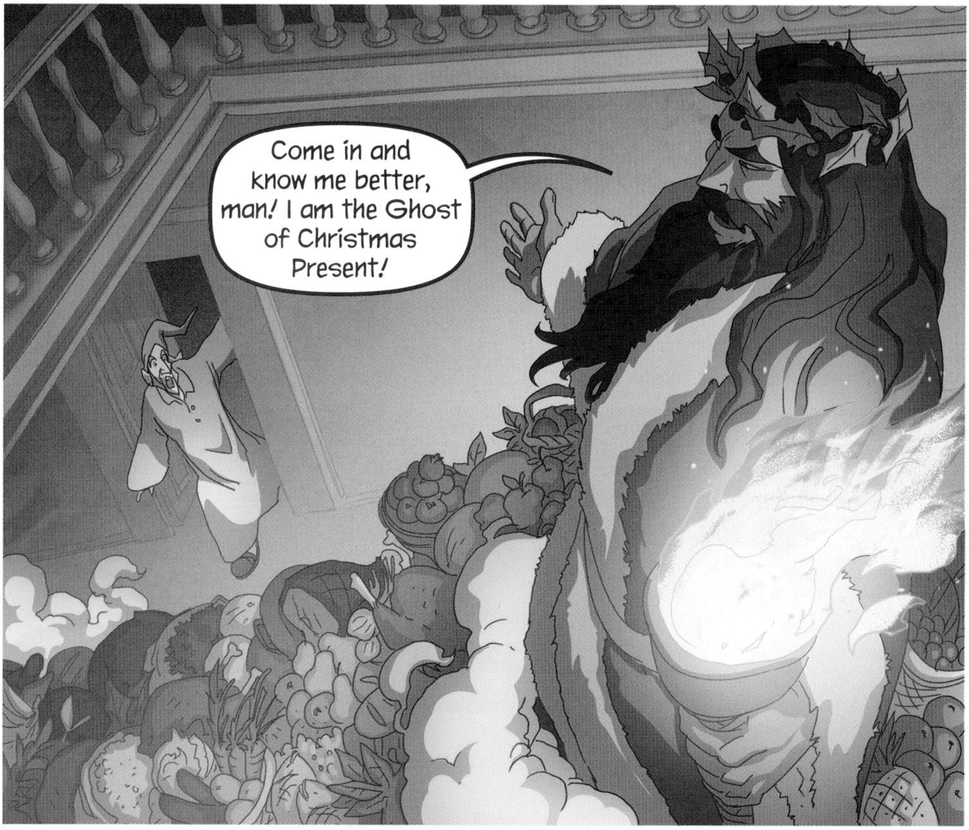
Come in and know me better, man! I am the Ghost of Christmas Present!

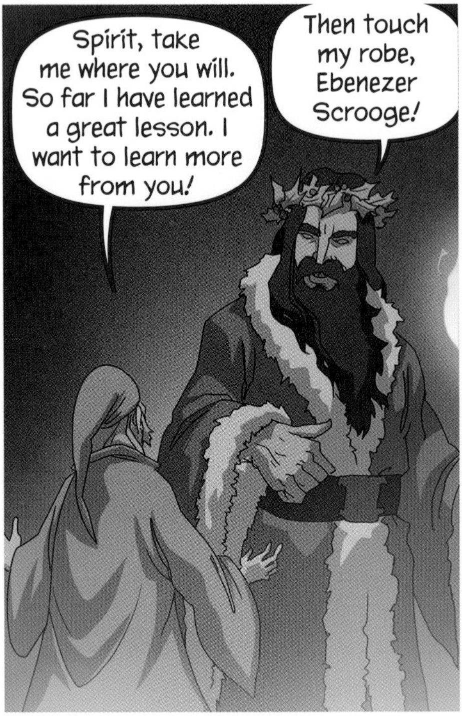
Spirit, take me where you will. So far I have learned a great lesson. I want to learn more from you!
Then touch my robe, Ebenezer Scrooge!

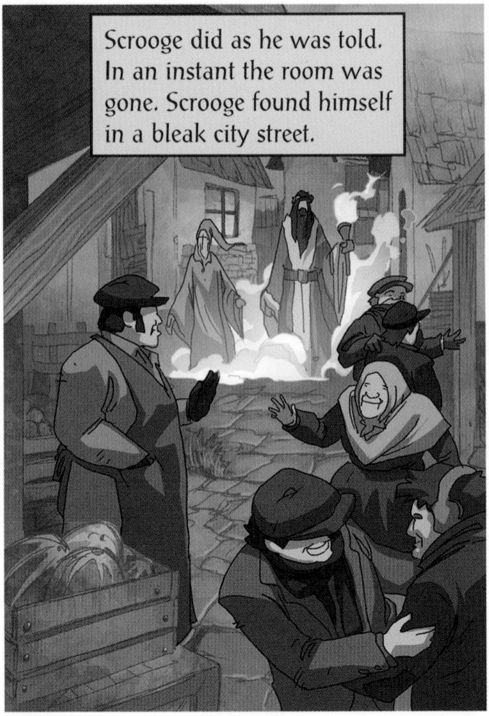
Scrooge did as he was told. In an instant the room was gone. Scrooge found himself in a bleak city street.

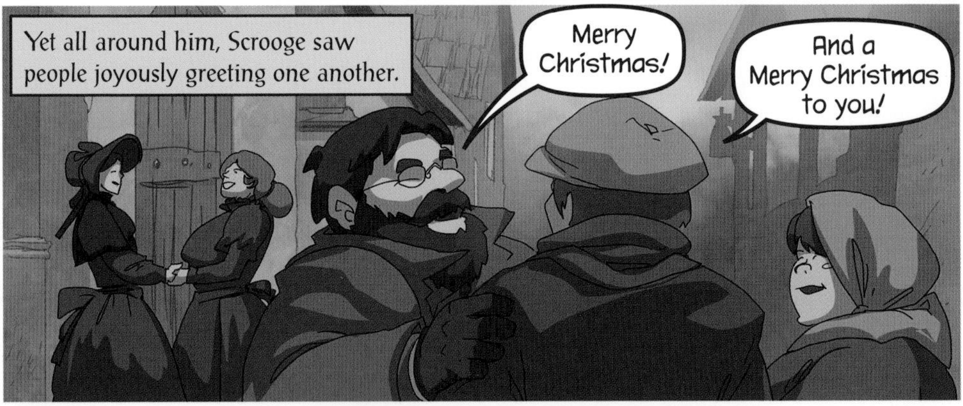
Yet all around him, Scrooge saw people joyously greeting one another.
Merry Christmas!
And a Merry Christmas to you!

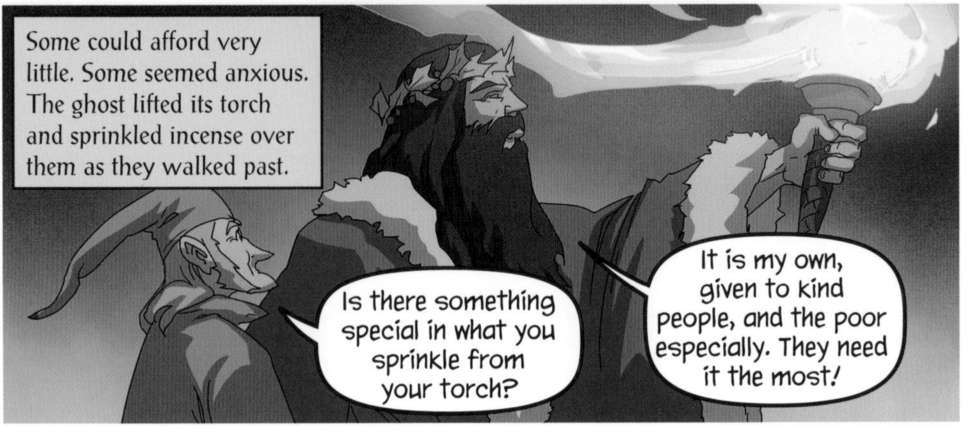
Some could afford very little. Some seemed anxious. The ghost lifted its torch and sprinkled incense over them as they walked past.
Is there something special in what you sprinkle from your torch?
It is my own, given to kind people, and the poor especially. They need it the most!

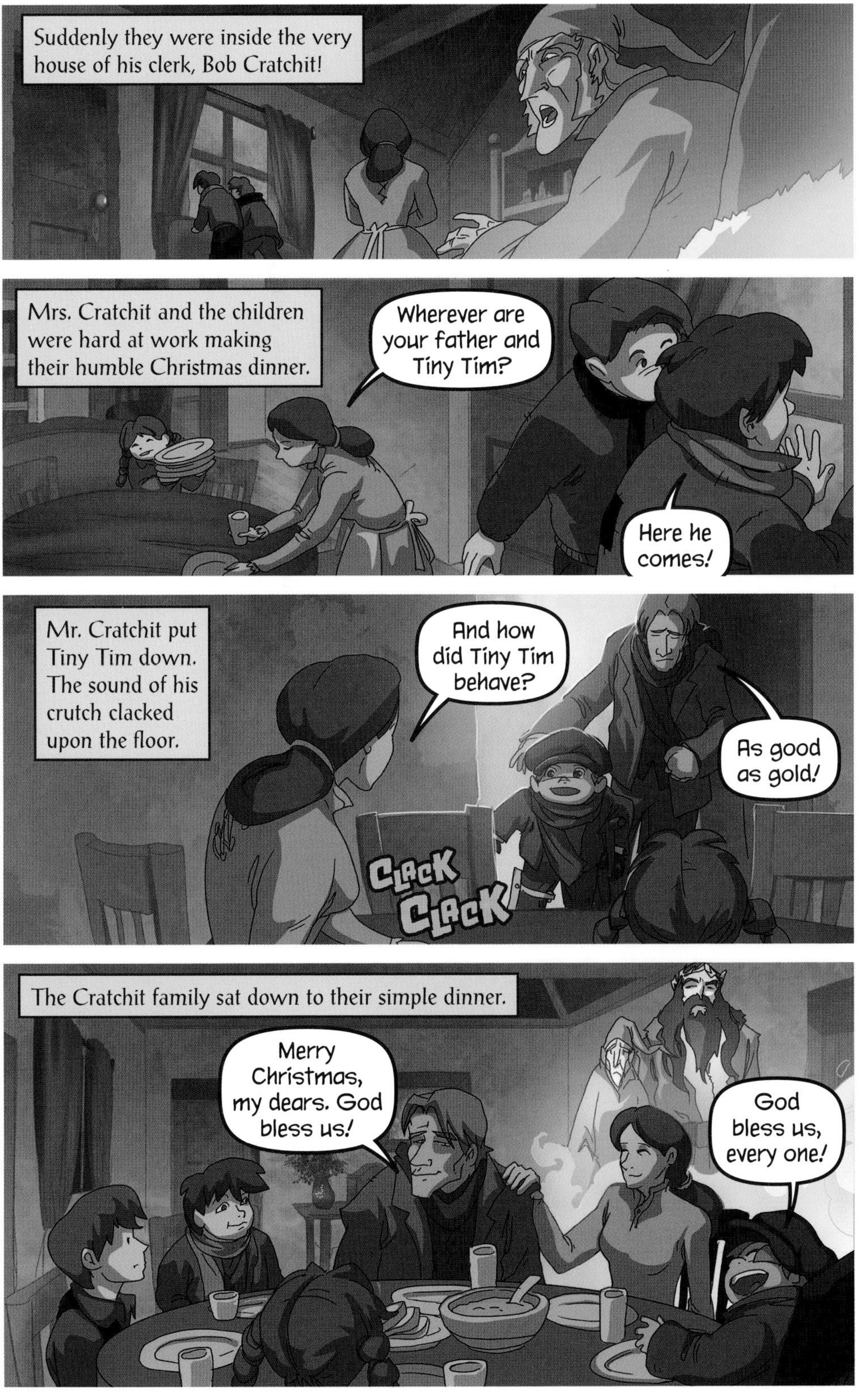
Suddenly they were inside the very house of his clerk, Bob Cratchit!
Mrs. Cratchit and the children were hard at work making their humble Christmas dinner.
Wherever are your father and Tiny Tim?
Here he comes!
Mr. Cratchit put Tiny Tim down. The sound of his crutch clacked upon the floor.
And how did Tiny Tim behave?
As good as gold!
CLACK
CLACK
The Cratchit family sat down to their simple dinner.
Merry Christmas, my dears. God bless us!
God bless us, every one!

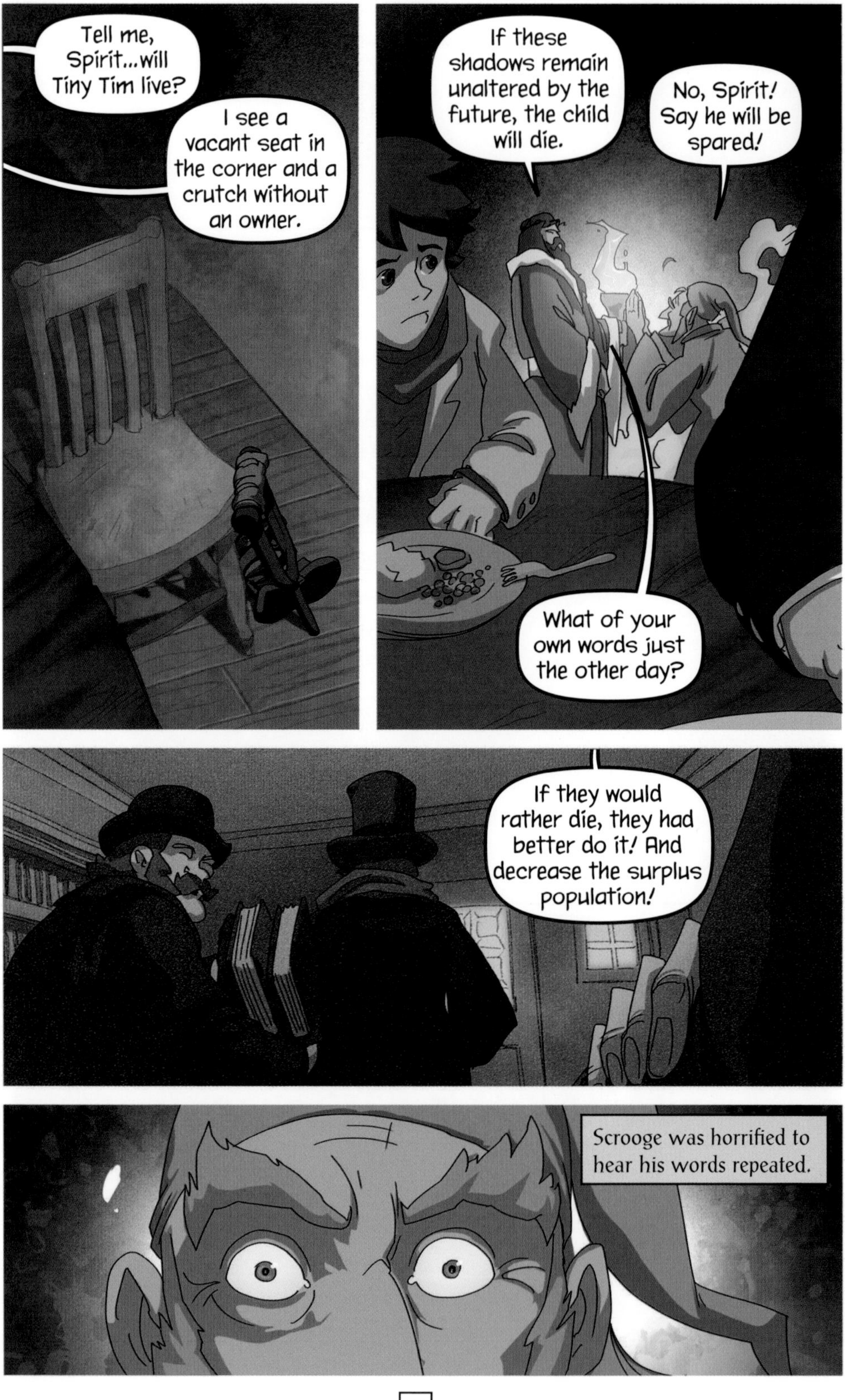
Tell me, Spirit...will Tiny Tim live?
I see a vacant seat in the corner and a crutch without an owner.
If these shadows remain unaltered by the future, the child will die.
No, Spirit! Say he will be spared!
What of your own words just the other day?
If they would rather die, they had better do it! And decrease the surplus population!
Scrooge was horrified to hear his words repeated.

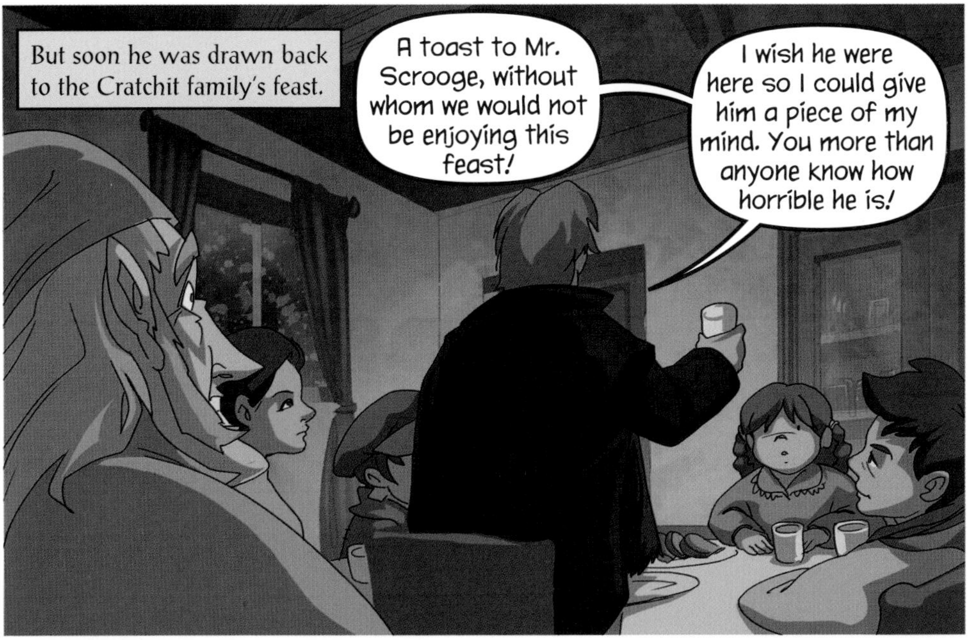
But soon he was drawn back to the Cratchit family's feast.
A toast to Mr. Scrooge, without whom we would not be enjoying this feast!
I wish he were here so I could give him a piece of my mind. You more than anyone know how horrible he is!

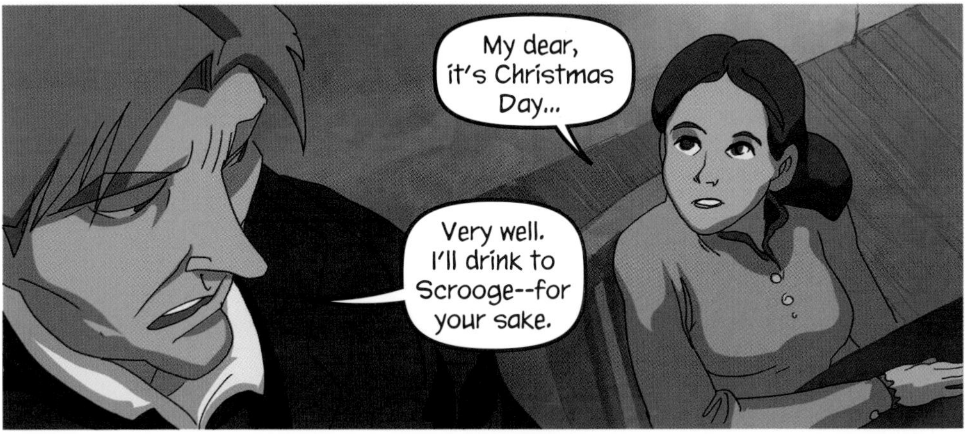
My dear, it's Christmas Day...
Very well. I'll drink to Scrooge--for your sake.

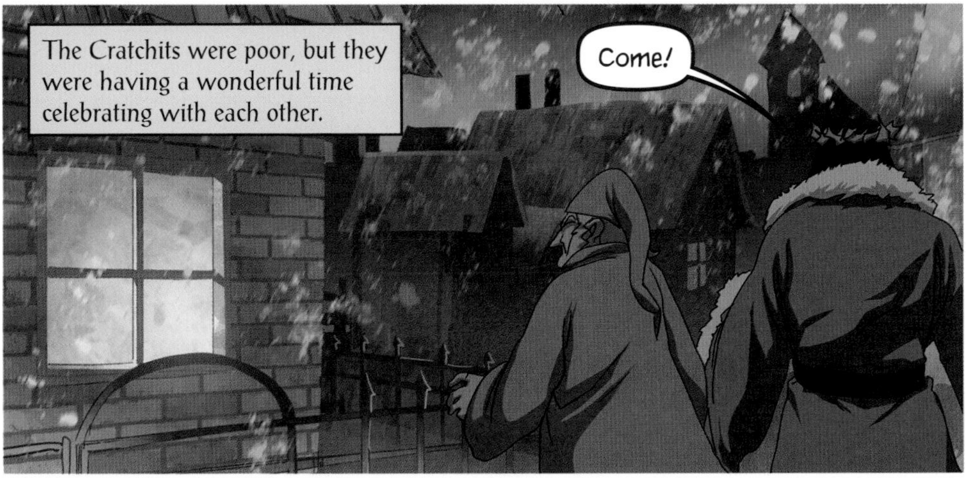
The Cratchits were poor, but they were having a wonderful time celebrating with each other.
Come!

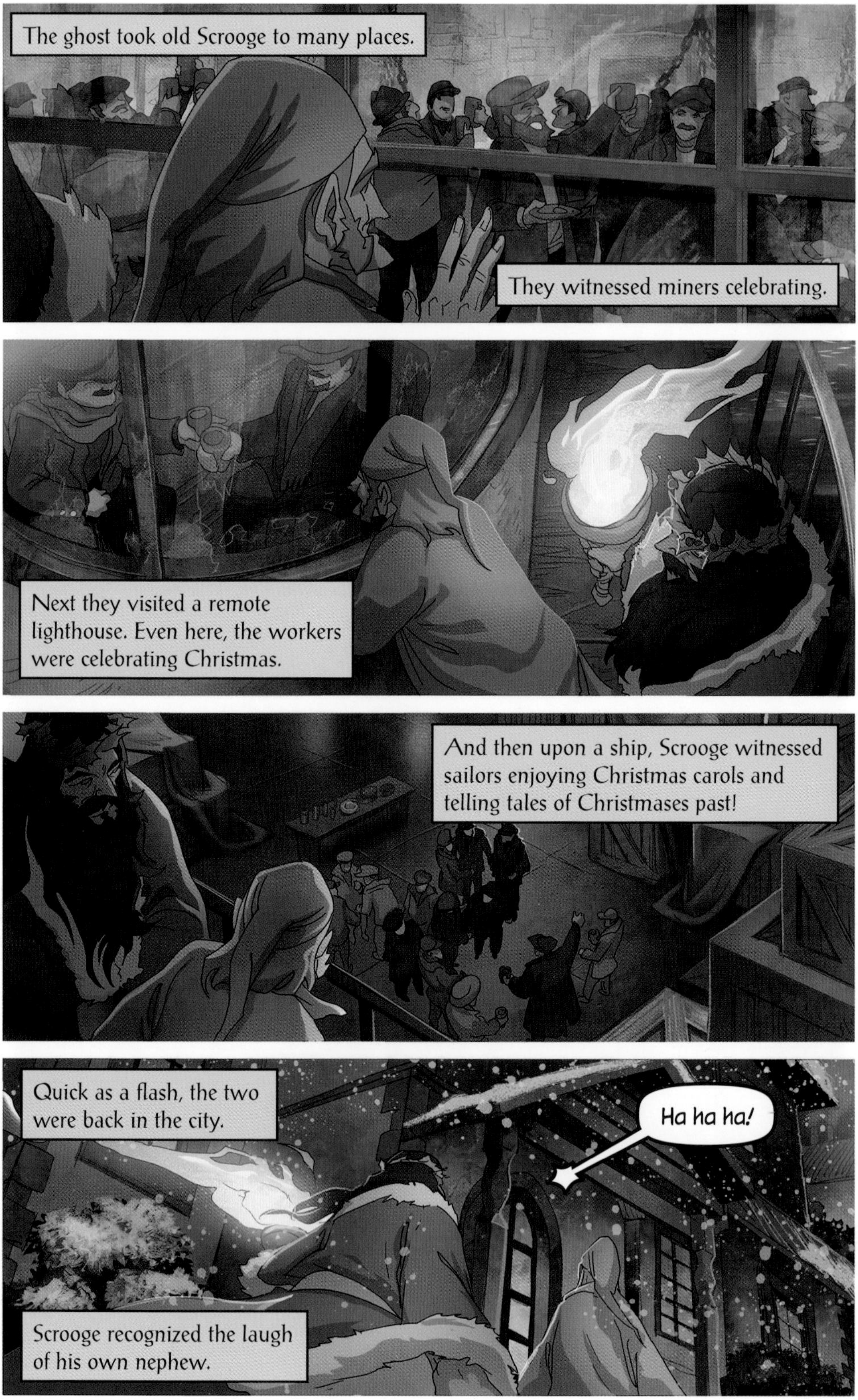
The ghost took old Scrooge to many places.
They witnessed miners celebrating.
Next they visited a remote lighthouse. Even here, the workers were celebrating Christmas.
And then upon a ship, Scrooge witnessed sailors enjoying Christmas carols and telling tales of Christmases past!
Quick as a flash, the two were back in the city.
Ha ha ha!
Scrooge recognized the laugh of his own nephew.

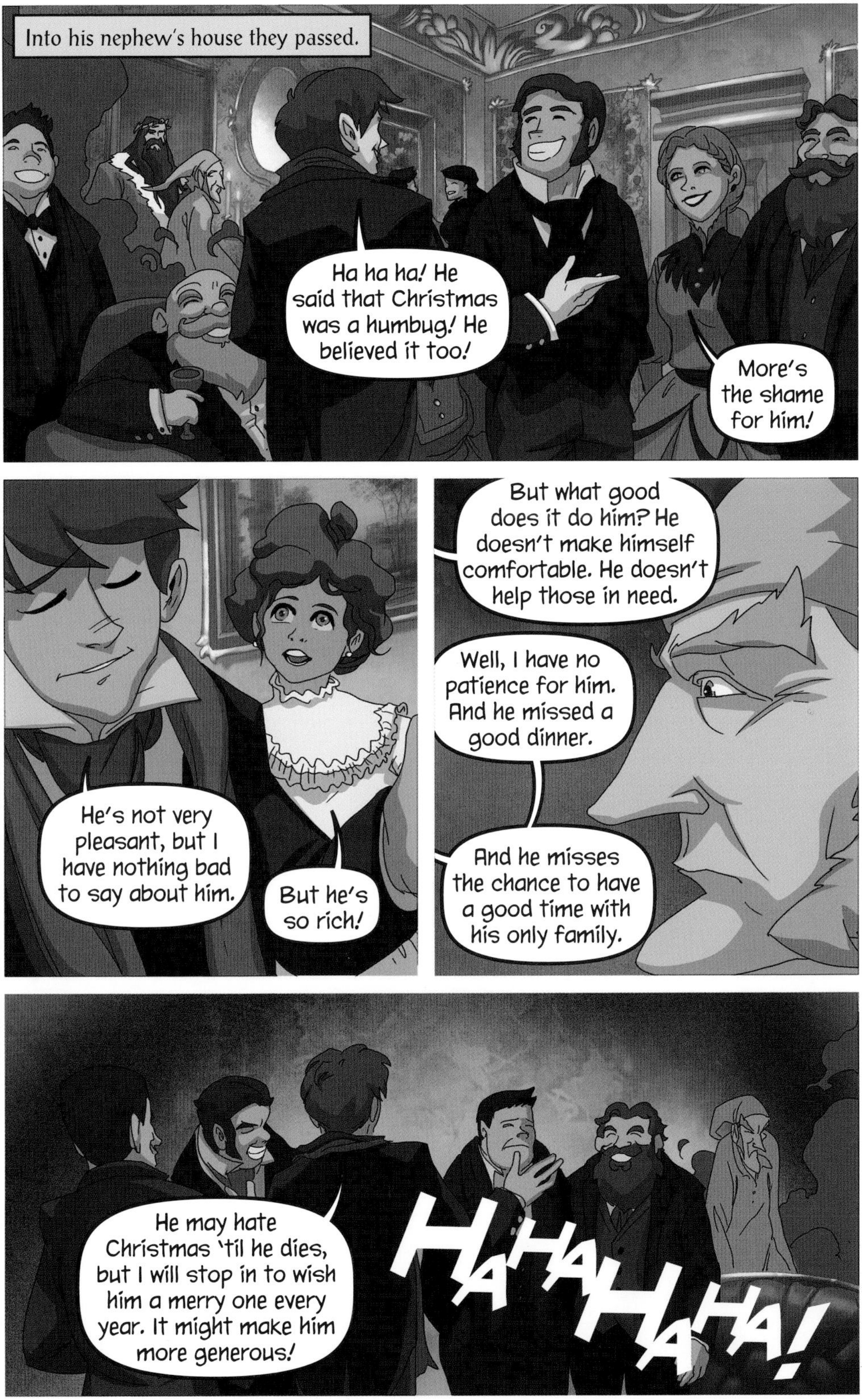
Into his nephew's house they passed.
Ha ha ha! He said that Christmas was a humbug! He believed it too!
More's the shame for him!
He's not very pleasant, but I have nothing bad to say about him.
But he's so rich!
But what good does it do him? He doesn't make himself comfortable. He doesn't help those in need.
Well, I have no patience for him. And he missed a good dinner.
And he misses the chance to have a good time with his only family.
He may hate Christmas 'til he dies, but I will stop in to wish him a merry one every year. It might make him more generous!
HA HA HA HA HA HA!

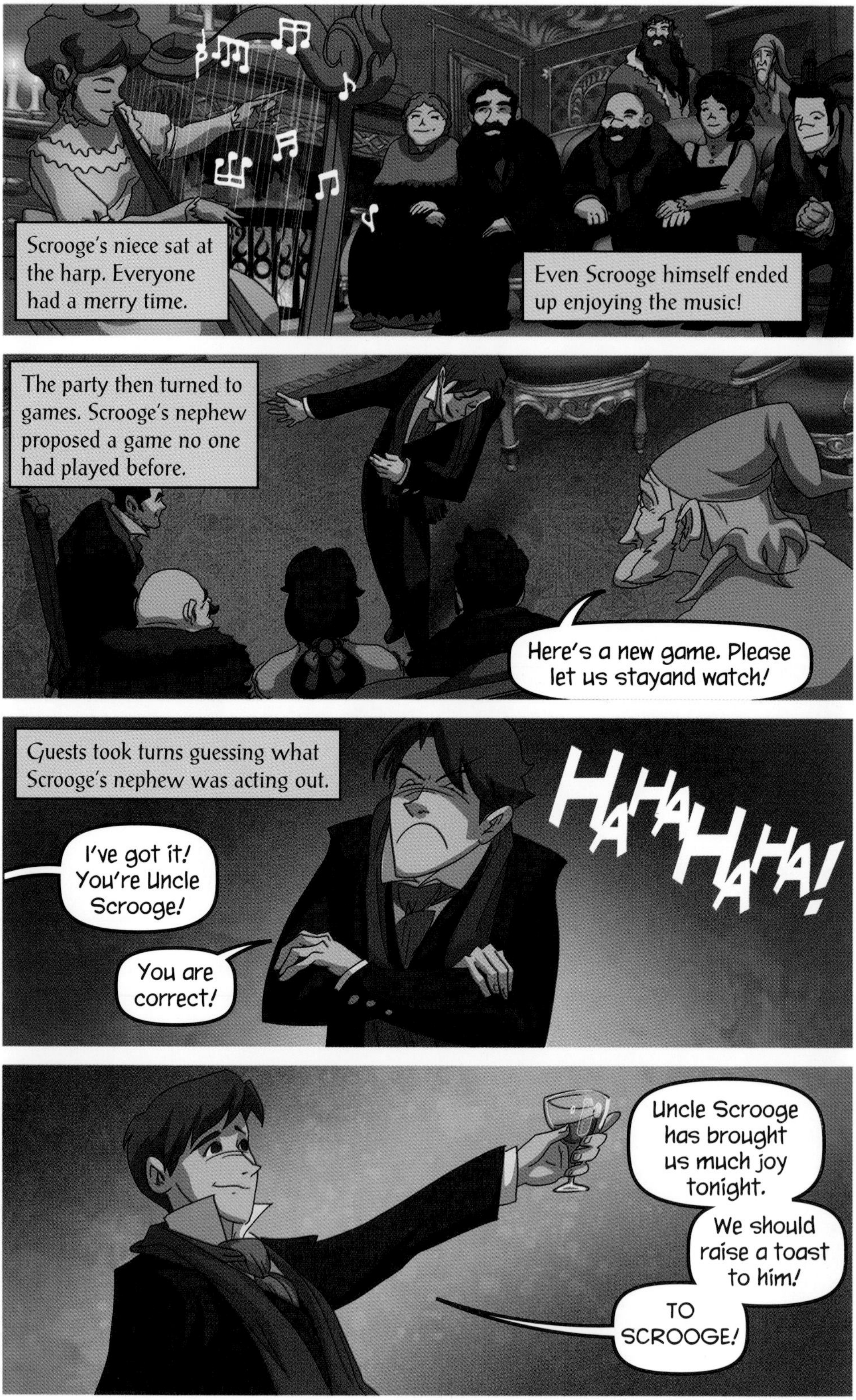
Scrooge's niece sat at the harp. Everyone had a merry time.
Even Scrooge himself ended up enjoying the music!
The party then turned to games. Scrooge's nephew proposed a game no one had played before.
Here's a new game. Please let us stayand watch!
Guests took turns guessing what Scrooge's nephew was acting out.
HAHAHAHA!
I've got it! You're Uncle Scrooge!
You are correct!
Uncle Scrooge has brought us much joy tonight.
We should raise a toast to him!
TO SCROOGE!

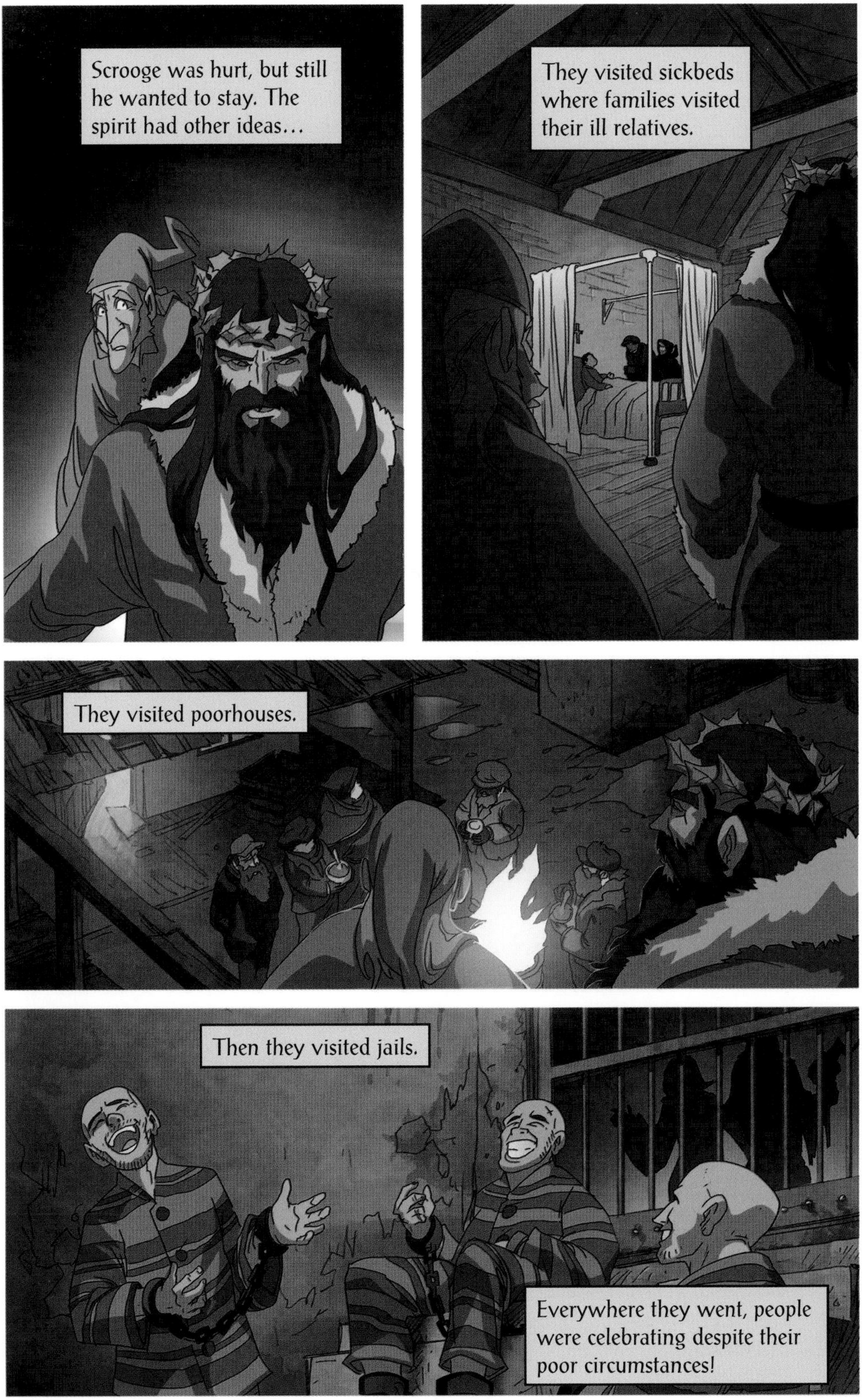
Scrooge was hurt, but still he wanted to stay. The spirit had other ideas...
They visited sickbeds where families visited their ill relatives.
They visited poorhouses.
Then they visited jails.
Everywhere they went, people were celebrating despite their poor circumstances!

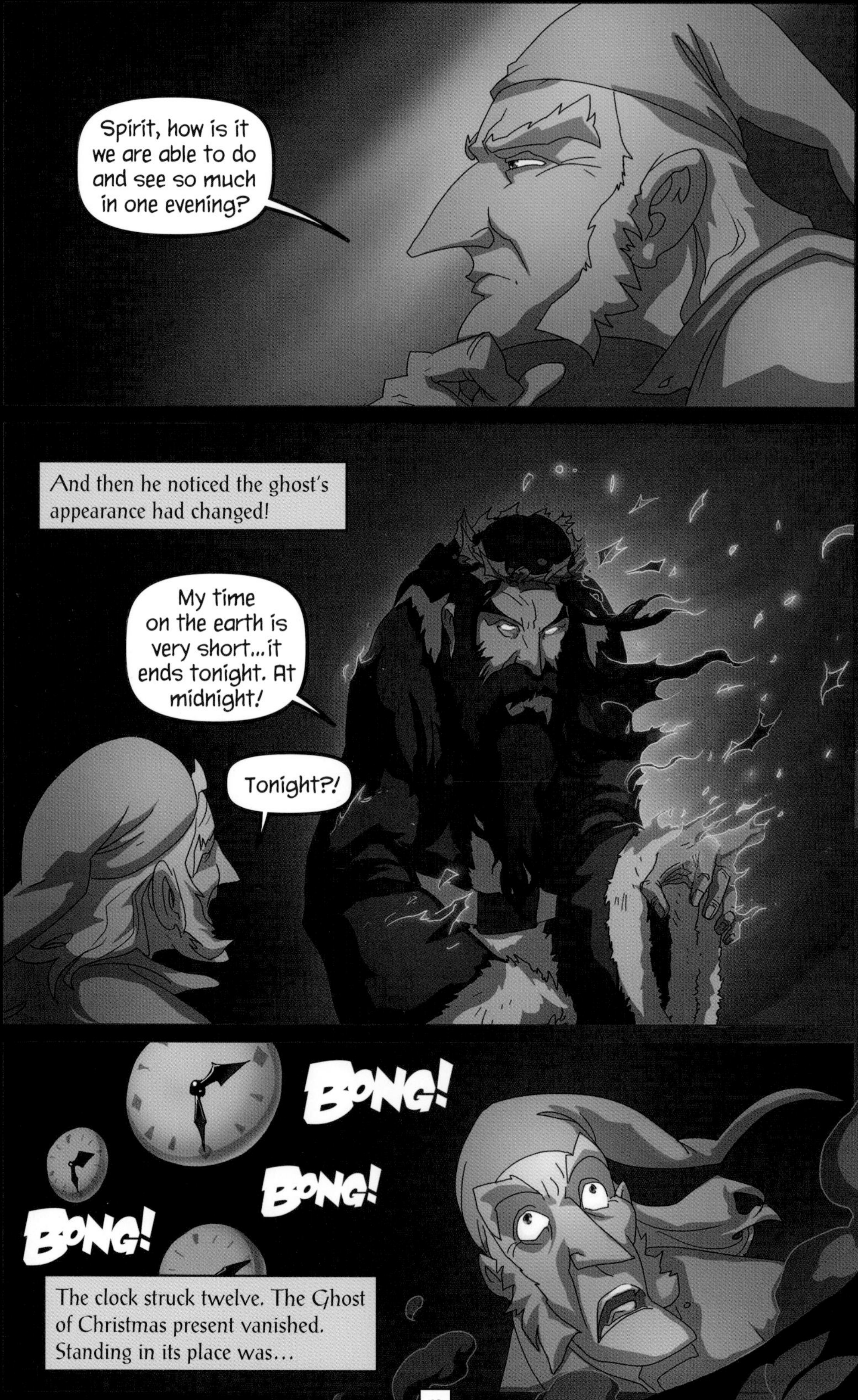
Spirit, how is it we are able to do and see so much in one evening?
And then he noticed the ghost's appearance had changed!
My time on the earth is very short...it ends tonight. At midnight!
Tonight?!
BONG!
BONG!
BONG!
The clock struck twelve. The Ghost of Christmas present vanished. Standing in its place was…

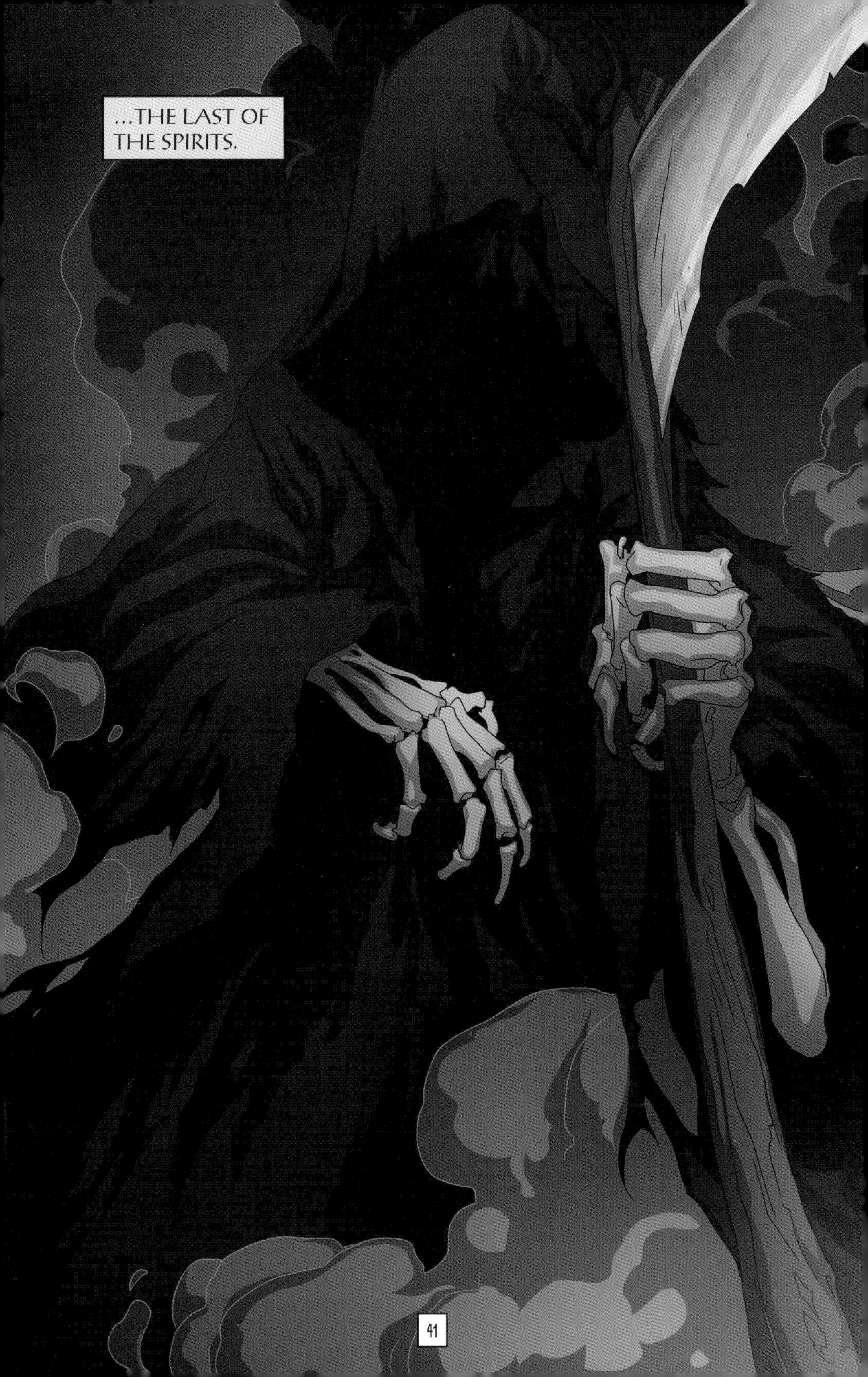
...THE LAST OF
THE SPIRITS.

CHAPTER 4
THE LAST OF THE SPIRITS

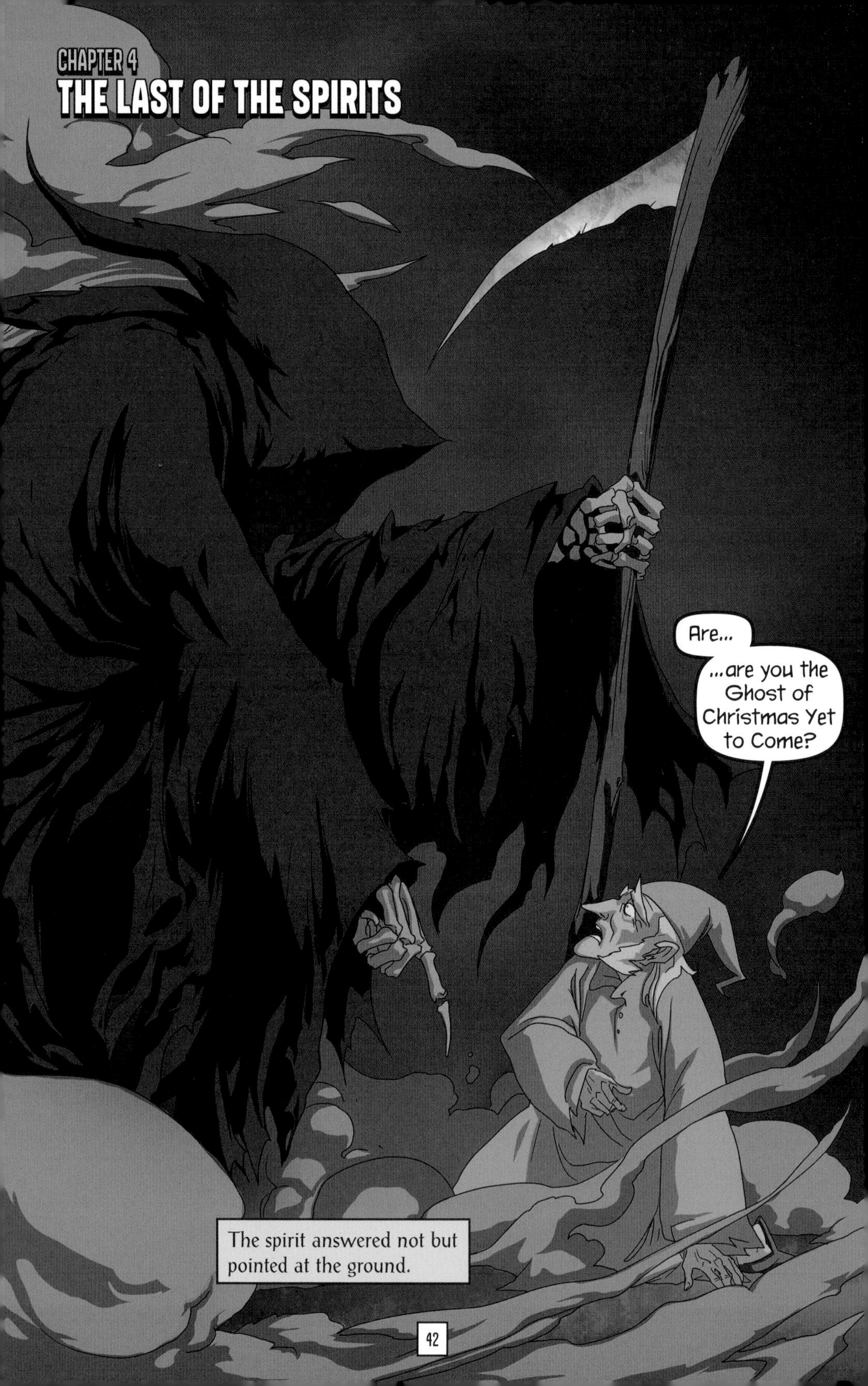
Are...
...are you the Ghost of Christmas Yet to Come?
The spirit answered not but pointed at the ground.

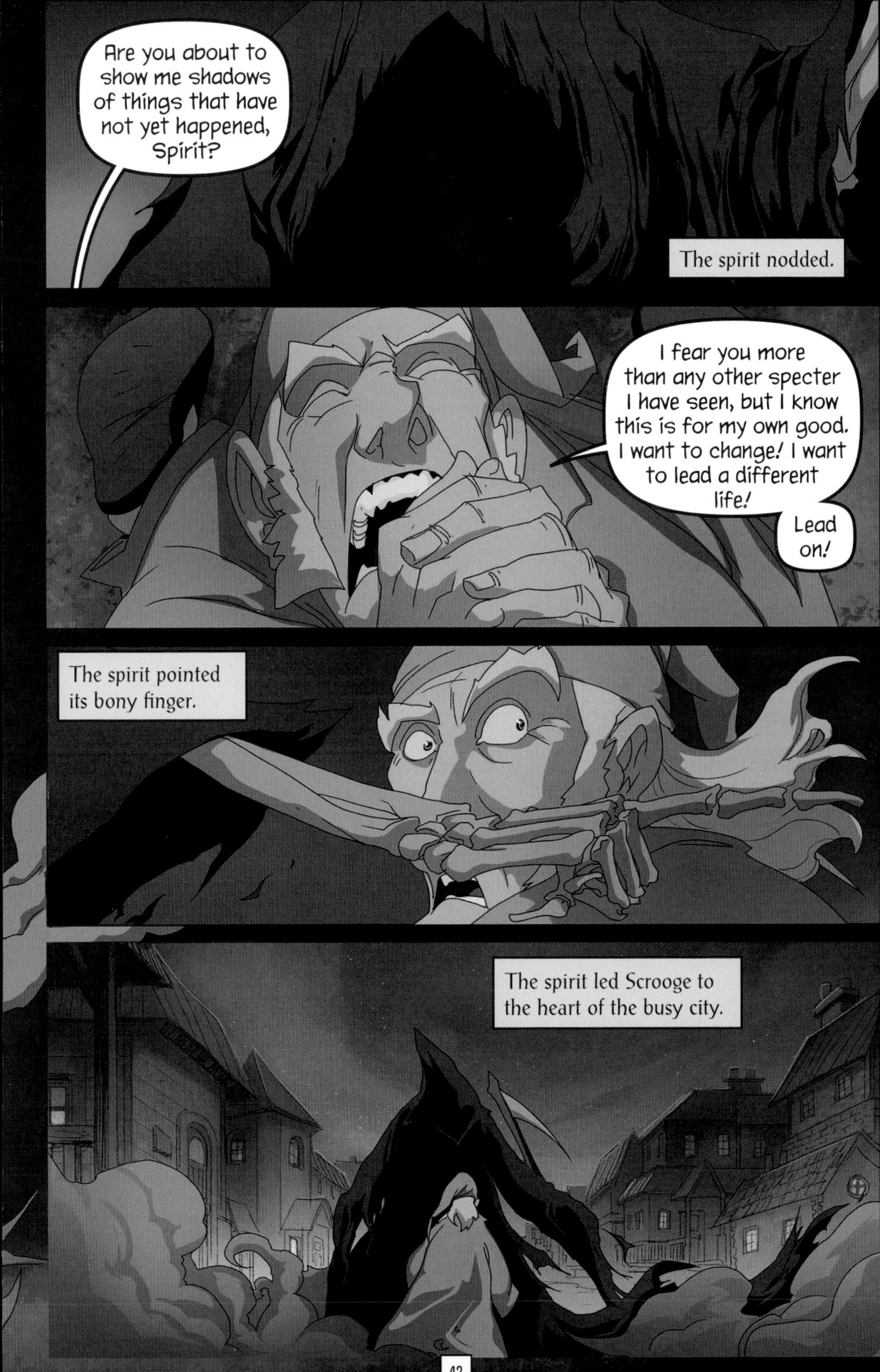
Are you about to show me shadows of things that have not yet happened, Spirit?
The spirit nodded.
I fear you more than any other specter I have seen, but I know this is for my own good. I want to change! I want to lead a different life!
Lead on!
The spirit pointed its bony finger.
The spirit led Scrooge to the heart of the busy city.

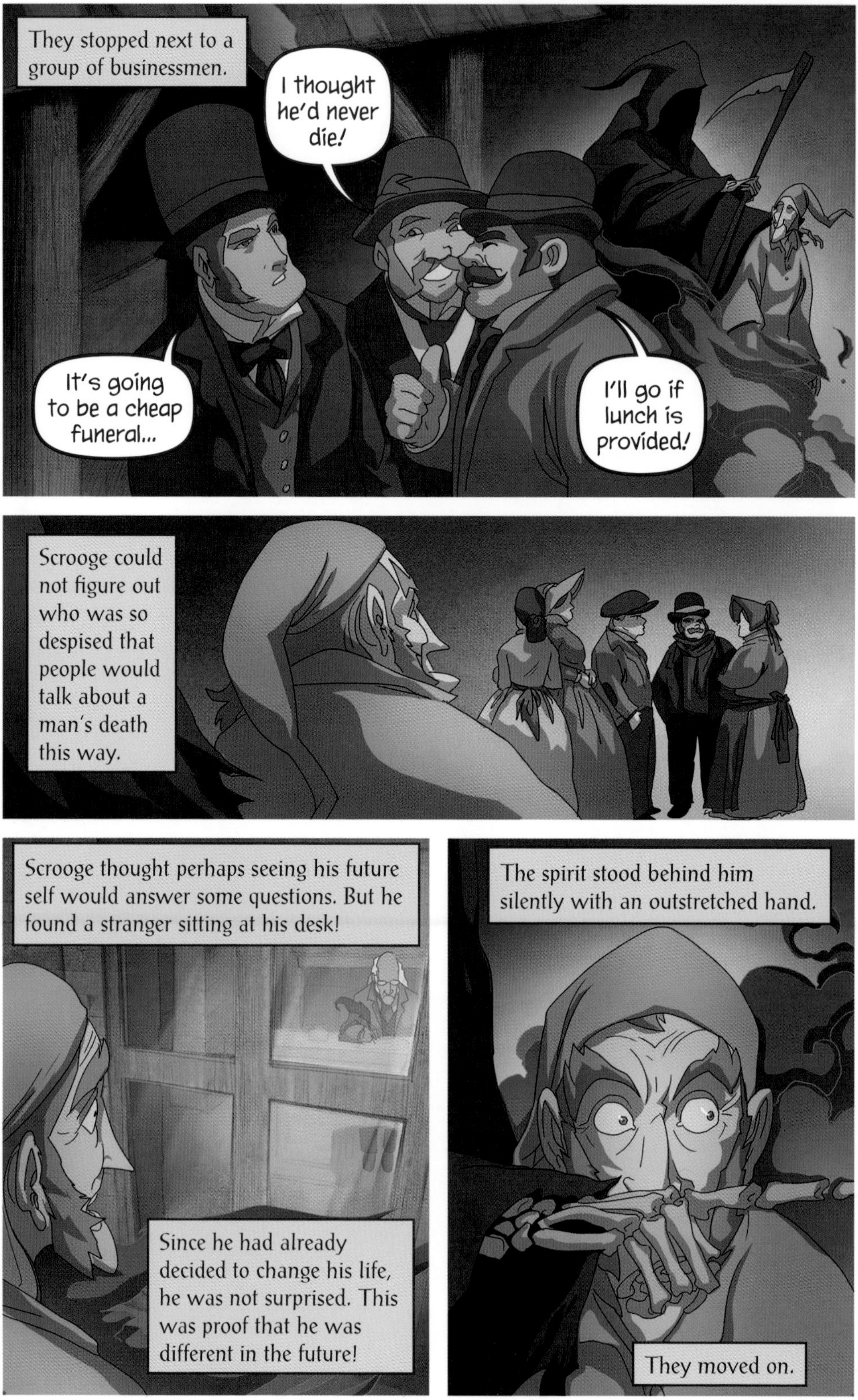
They stopped next to a group of businessmen.
I thought he'd never die!
It's going to be a cheap funeral...
I'll go if lunch is provided!
Scrooge could not figure out who was so despised that people would talk about a man's death this way.
Scrooge thought perhaps seeing his future self would answer some questions. But he found a stranger sitting at his desk!
Since he had already decided to change his life, he was not surprised. This was proof that he was different in the future!
The spirit stood behind him silently with an outstretched hand.
They moved on.

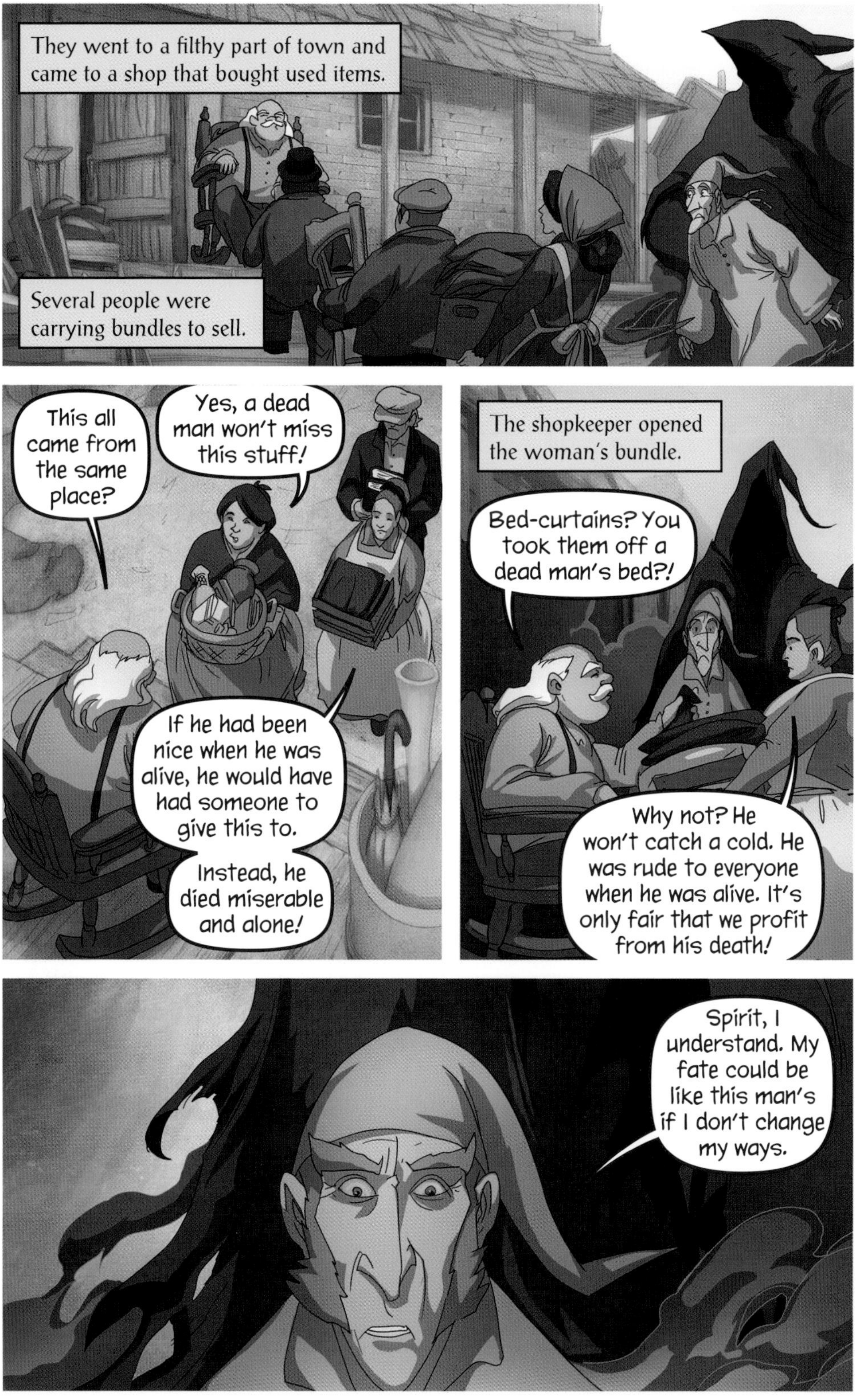

They went to a filthy part of town and came to a shop that bought used items.
Several people were carrying bundles to sell.
This all came from the same place?
Yes, a dead man won't miss this stuff!
If he had been nice when he was alive, he would have had someone to give this to.
Instead, he died miserable and alone!
The shopkeeper opened the woman's bundle.
Bed-curtains? You took them off a dead man's bed?!
Why not? He won't catch a cold. He was rude to everyone when he was alive. It's only fair that we profit from his death!
Spirit, I understand. My fate could be like this man's if I don't change my ways.

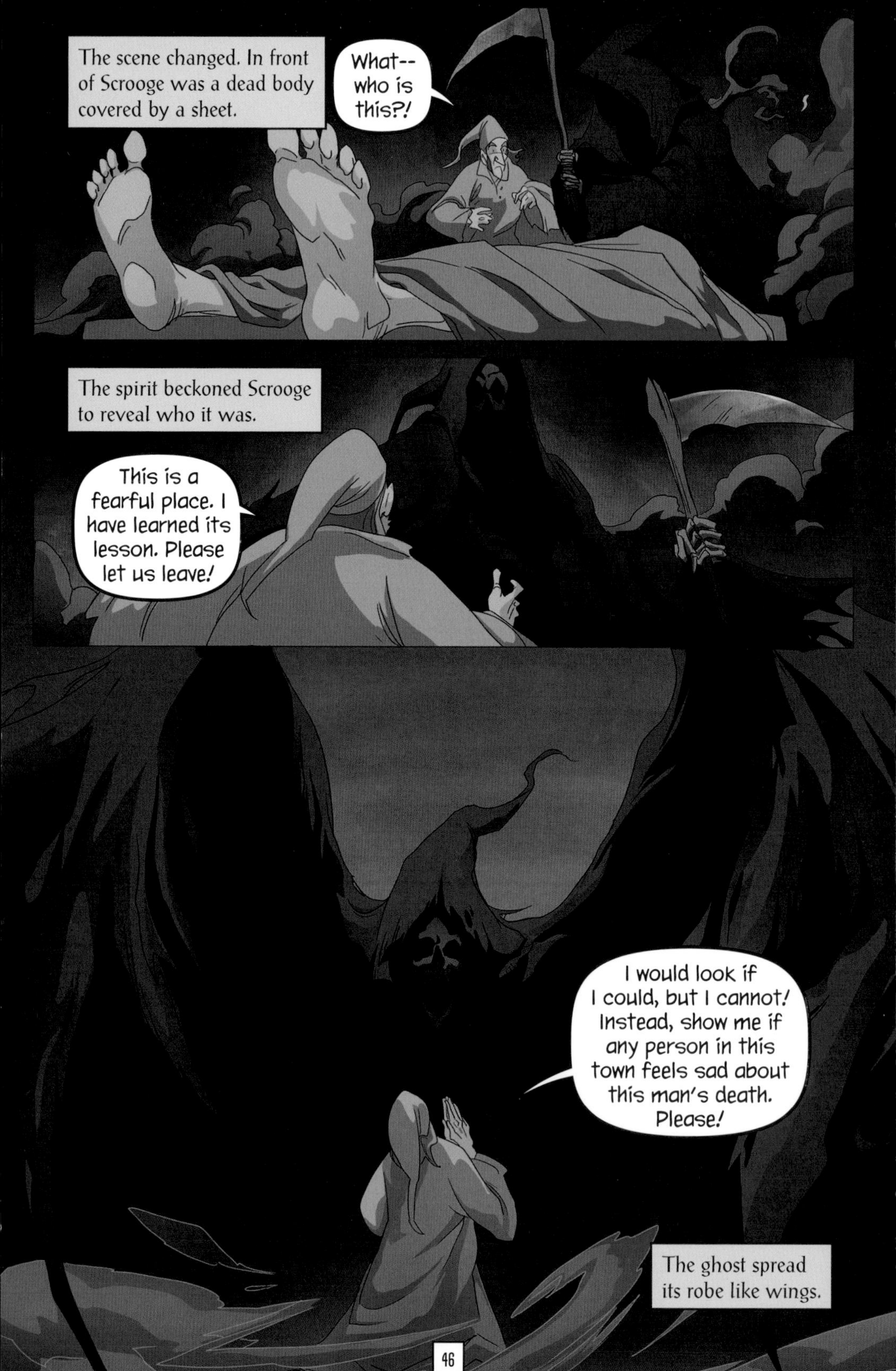
The scene changed. In front of Scrooge was a dead body covered by a sheet.
What-- who is this?!
The spirit beckoned Scrooge to reveal who it was.
This is a fearful place. I have learned its lesson. Please let us leave!
I would look if I could, but I cannot! Instead, show me if any person in this town feels sad about this man's death. Please!
The ghost spread its robe like wings.

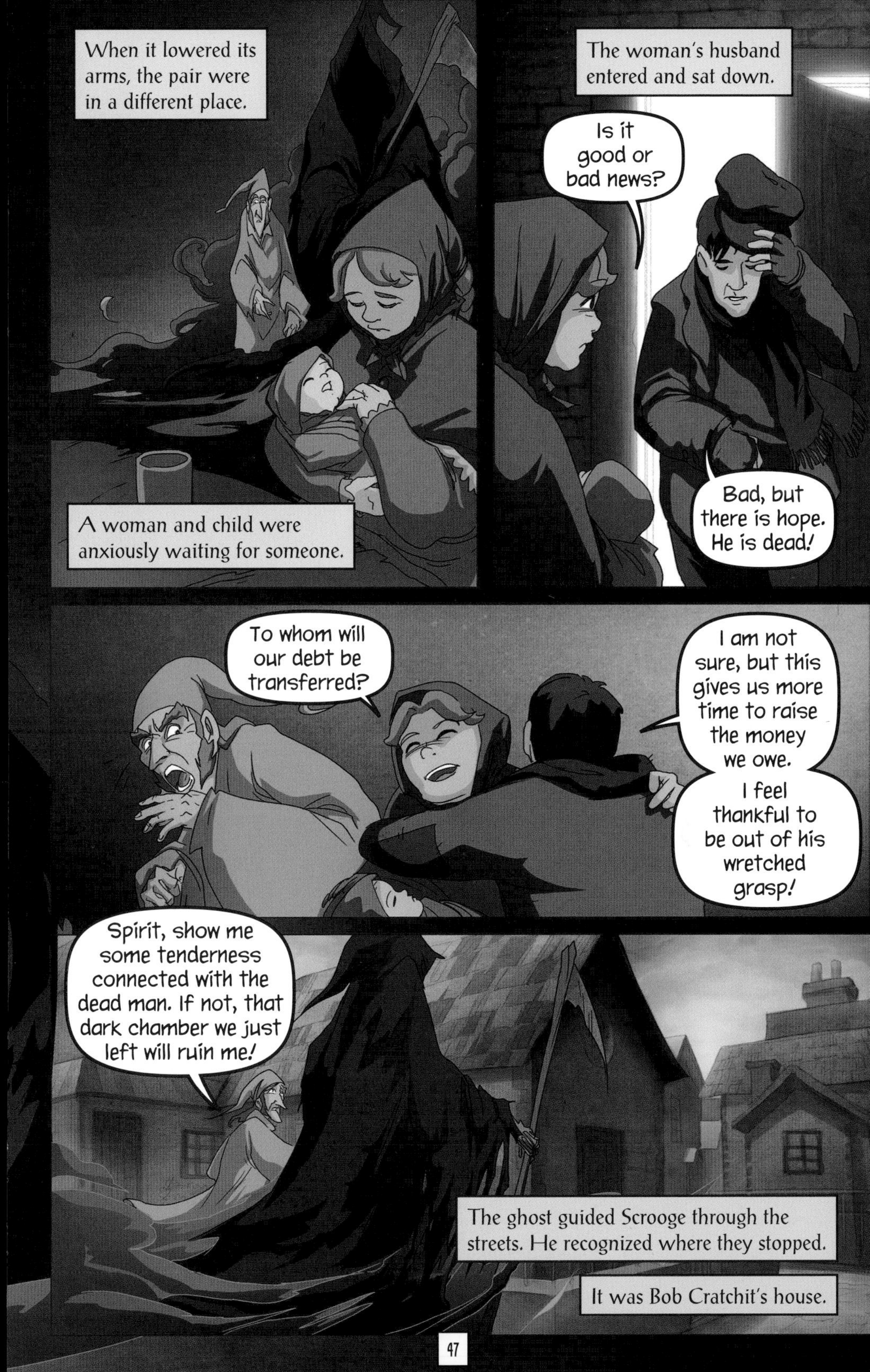
When it lowered its arms, the pair were in a different place.
A woman and child were anxiously waiting for someone.
The woman's husband entered and sat down.
Is it good or bad news?
Bad, but there is hope. He is dead!
To whom will our debt be transferred?
I am not sure, but this gives us more time to raise the money we owe.
I feel thankful to be out of his wretched grasp!
Spirit, show me some tenderness connected with the dead man. If not, that dark chamber we just left will ruin me!
The ghost guided Scrooge through the streets. He recognized where they stopped.
It was Bob Cratchit's house.

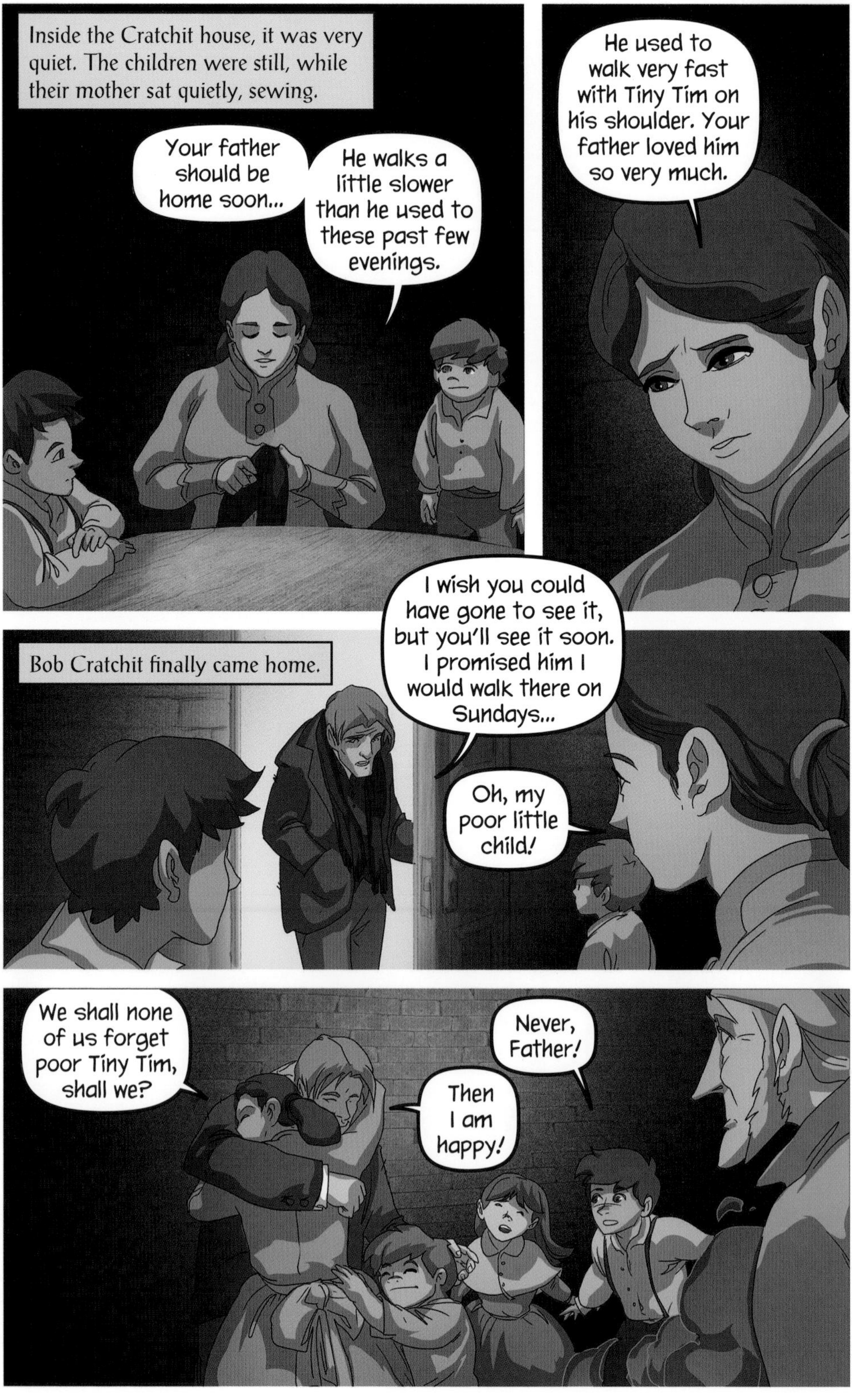

Inside the Cratchit house, it was very quiet. The children were still, while their mother sat quietly, sewing.
Your father should be home soon...
He walks a little slower than he used to these past few evenings.
He used to walk very fast with Tiny Tim on his shoulder. Your father loved him so very much.
Bob Cratchit finally came home.
I wish you could have gone to see it, but you'll see it soon. I promised him I would walk there on Sundays...
Oh, my poor little child!
We shall none of us forget poor Tiny Tim, shall we?
Never, Father!
Then I am happy!

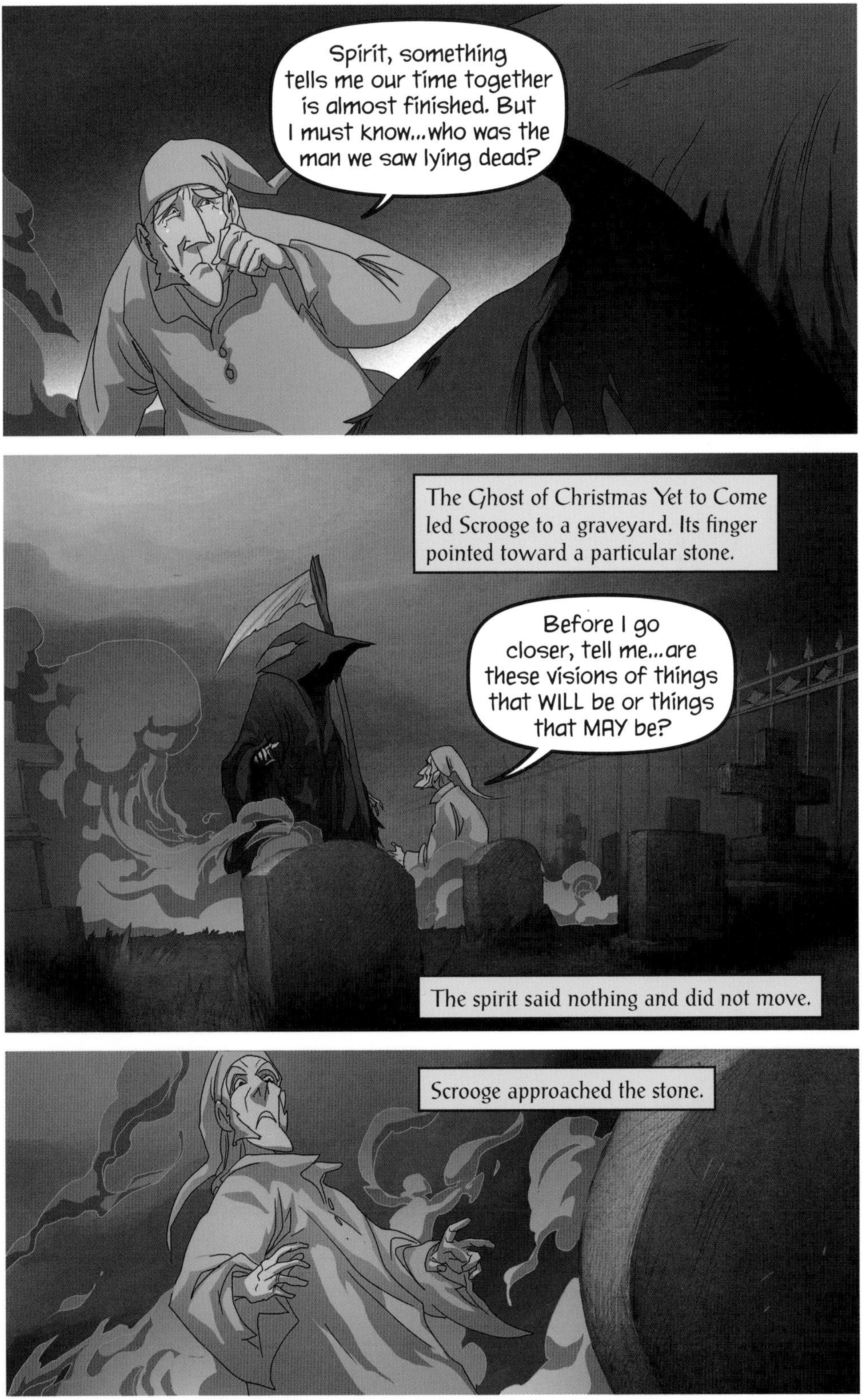
Spirit, something tells me our time together is almost finished. But I must know...who was the man we saw lying dead?
The Ghost of Christmas Yet to Come led Scrooge to a graveyard. Its finger pointed toward a particular stone.
Before I go closer, tell me...are these visions of things that WILL be or things that MAY be?
The spirit said nothing and did not move.
Scrooge approached the stone.

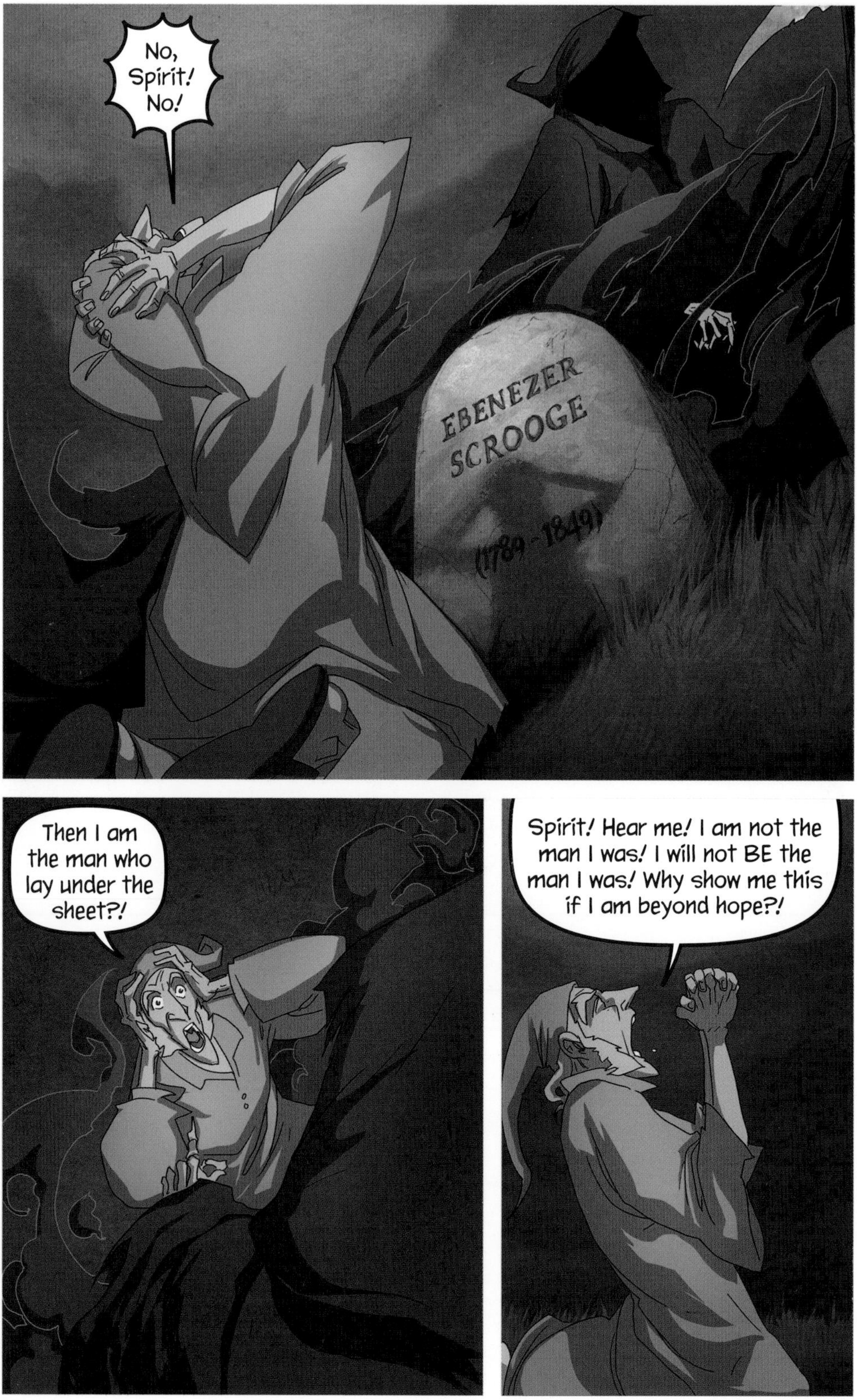
No, Spirit! No!
EBENEZER SCROOGE
(1789 - 1849)
Then I am the man who lay under the sheet?!
Spirit! Hear me! I am not the man I was! I will not BE the man I was! Why show me this if I am beyond hope?!

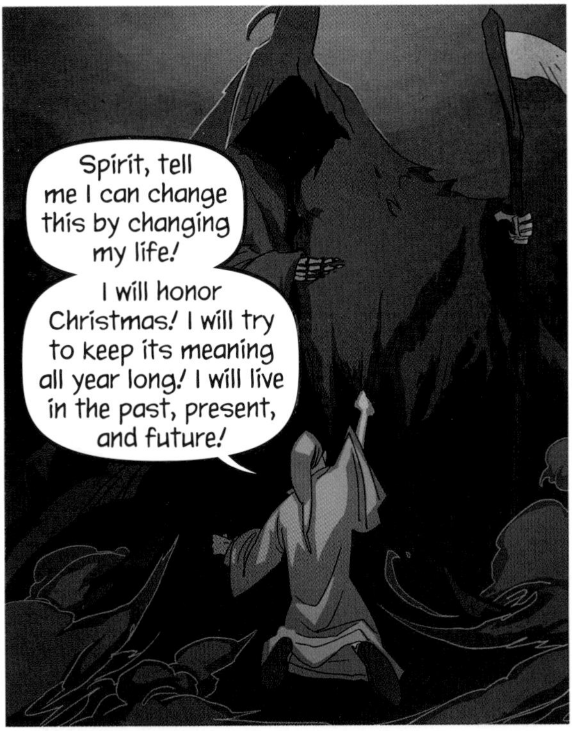
Spirit, tell me I can change this by changing my life!
I will honor Christmas! I will try to keep its meaning all year long! I will live in the past, present, and future!

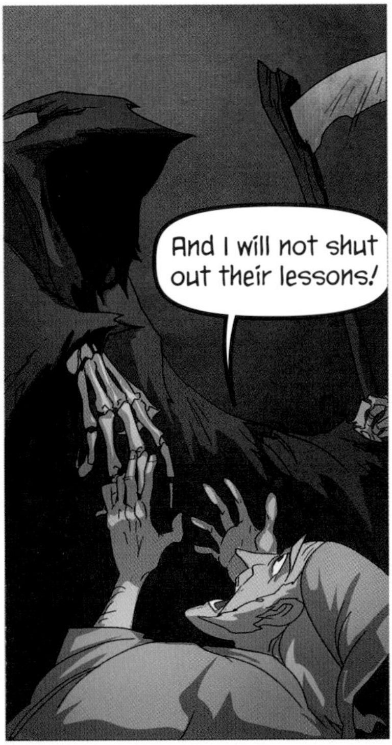
And I will not shut out their lessons!

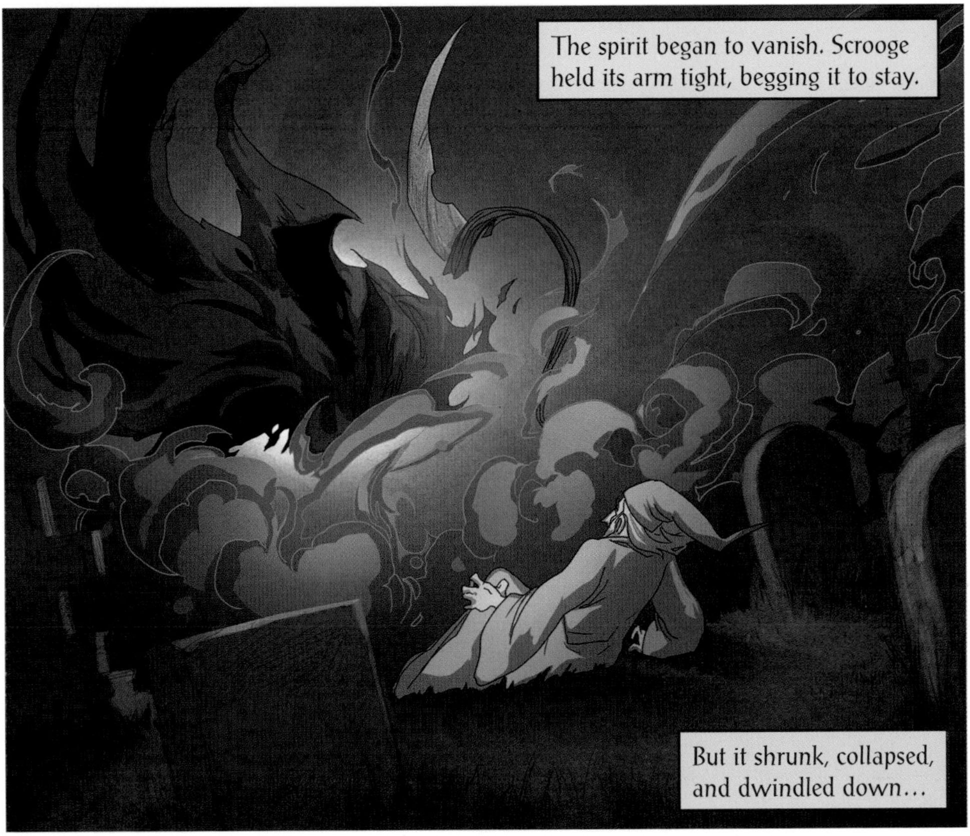
The spirit began to vanish. Scrooge held its arm tight, begging it to stay.
But it shrunk, collapsed, and dwindled down…

CHAPTER 5
THE END OF IT

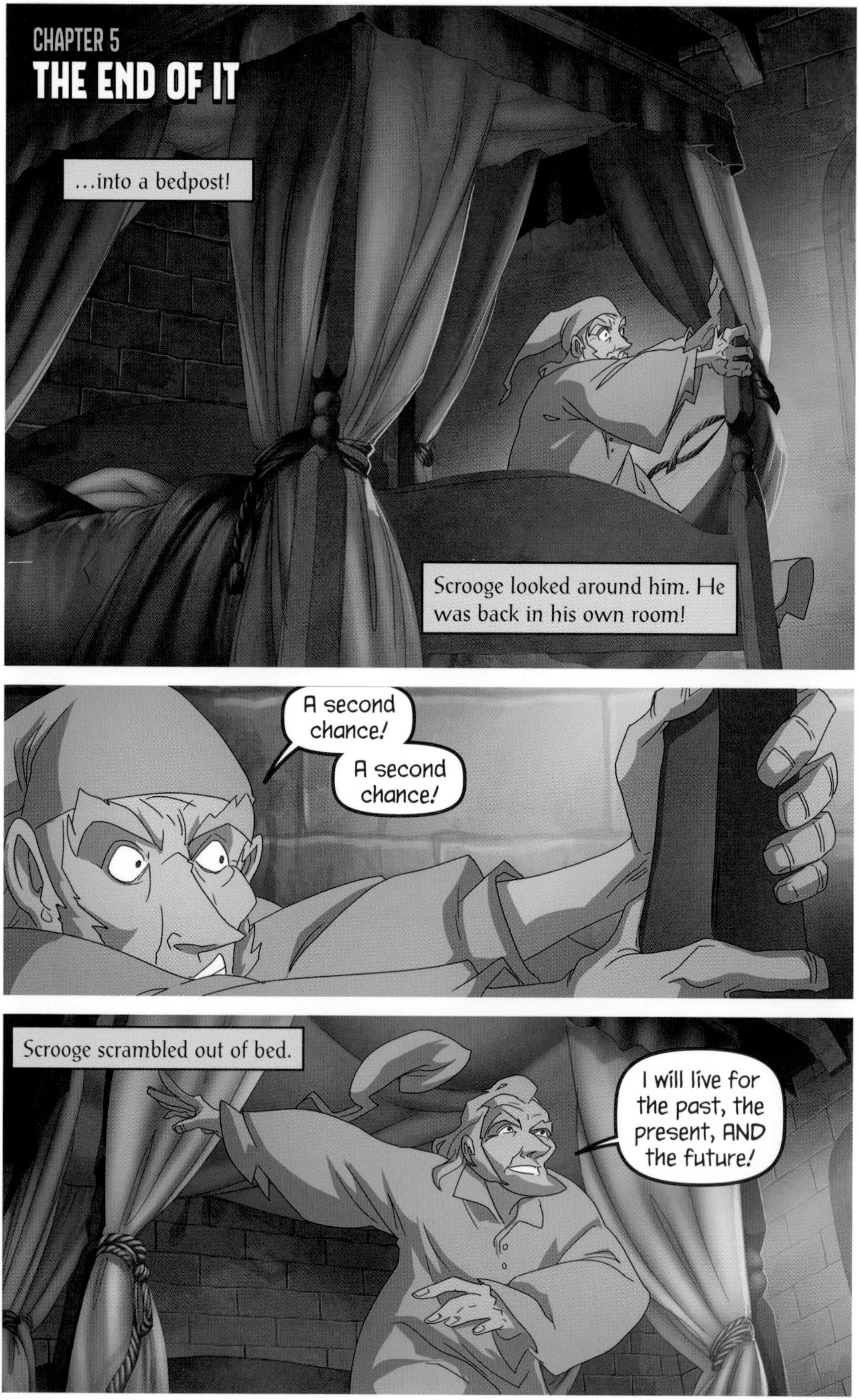
...into a bedpost!
Scrooge looked around him. He was back in his own room!
A second chance!
A second chance!
Scrooge scrambled out of bed.
I will live for the past, the present, AND the future!

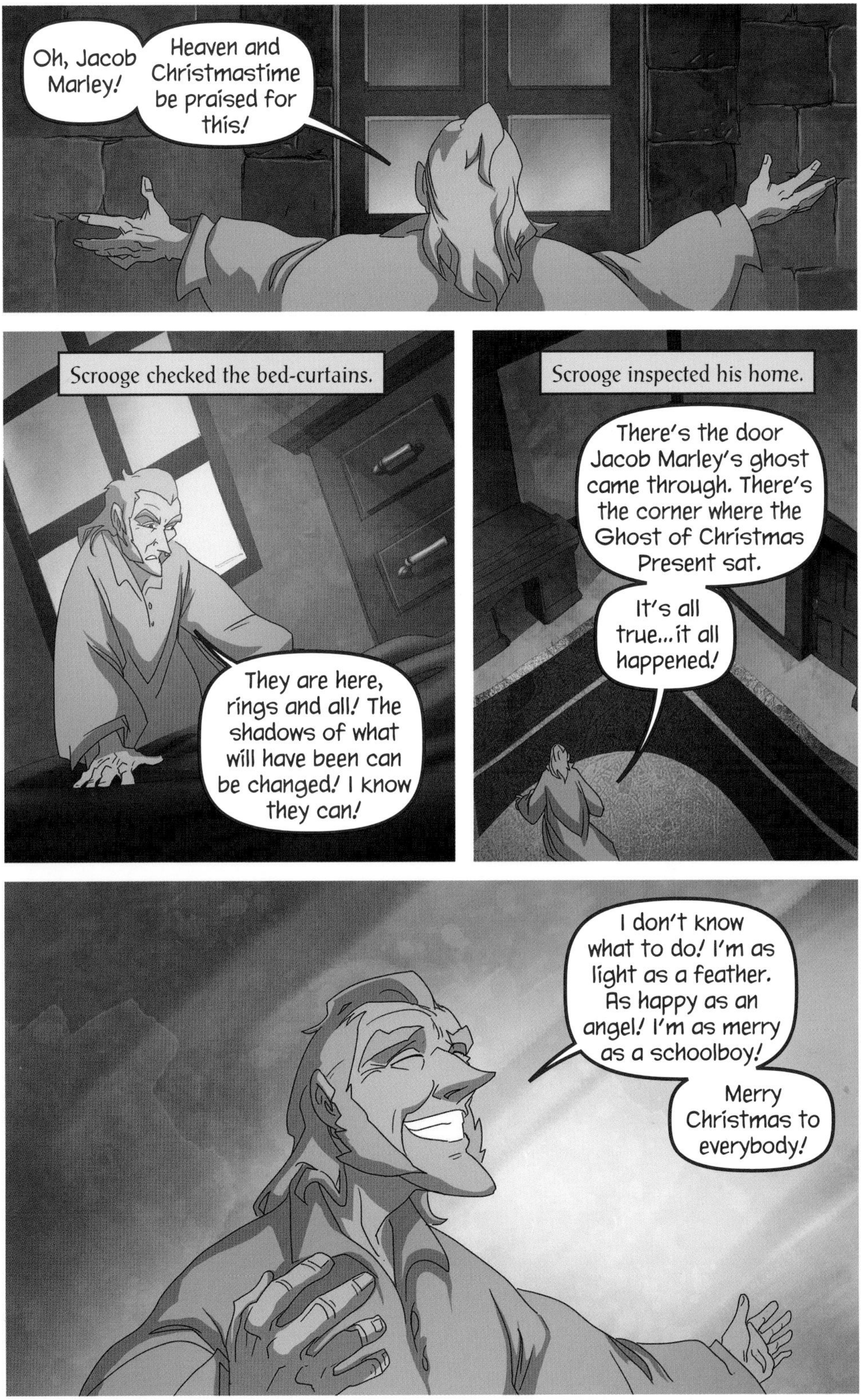
Oh, Jacob Marley!
Heaven and Christmastime be praised for this!
Scrooge checked the bed-curtains.
They are here, rings and all! The shadows of what will have been can be changed! I know they can!
Scrooge inspected his home.
There's the door Jacob Marley's ghost came through. There's the corner where the Ghost of Christmas Present sat.
It's all true...it all happened!
I don't know what to do! I'm as light as a feather. As happy as an angel! I'm as merry as a schoolboy!
Merry Christmas to everybody!

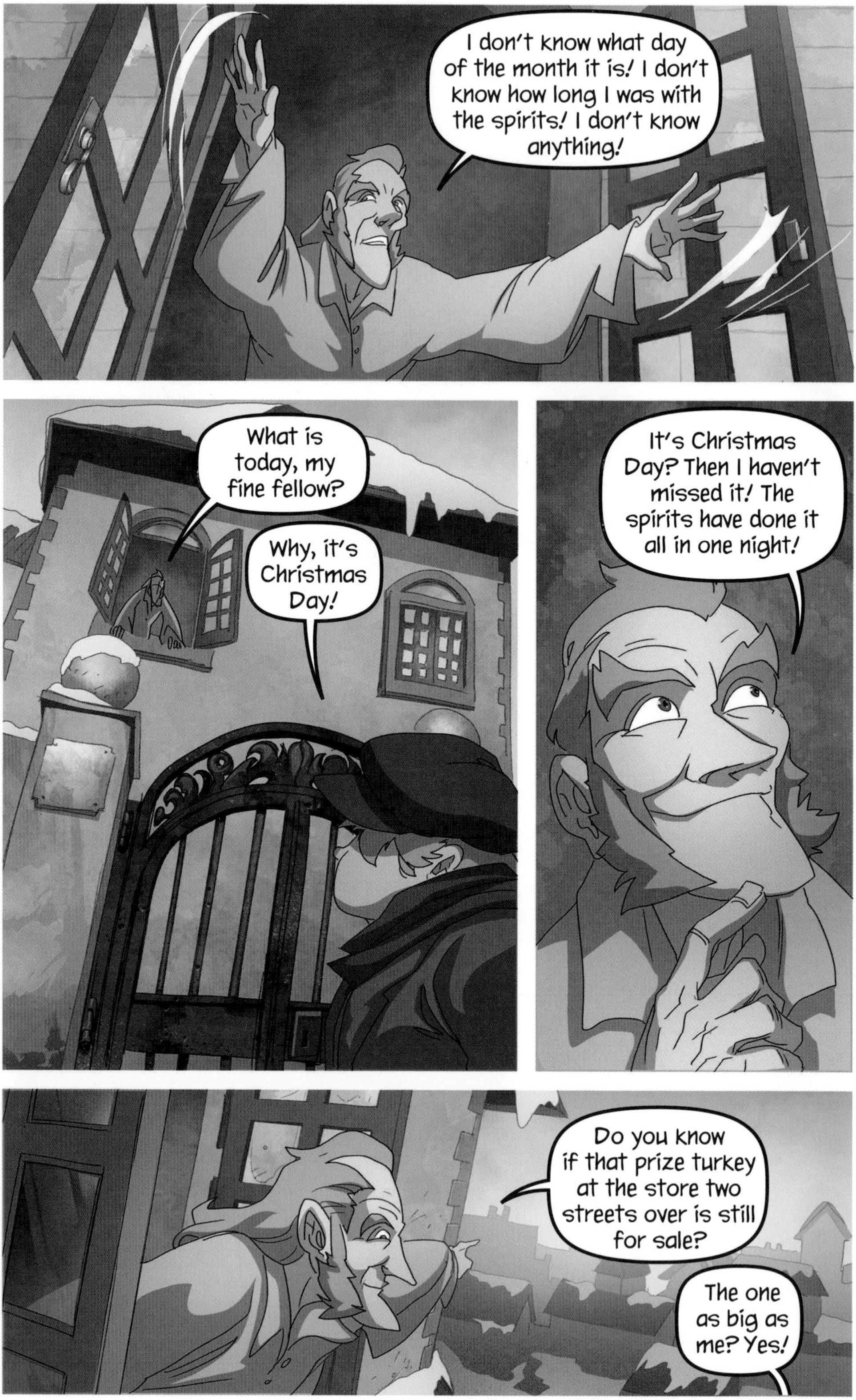
I don't know what day of the month it is! I don't know how long I was with the spirits! I don't know anything!
What is today, my fine fellow?
Why, it's Christmas Day!
It's Christmas Day? Then I haven't missed it! The spirits have done it all in one night!
Do you know if that prize turkey at the store two streets over is still for sale?
The one as big as me? Yes!

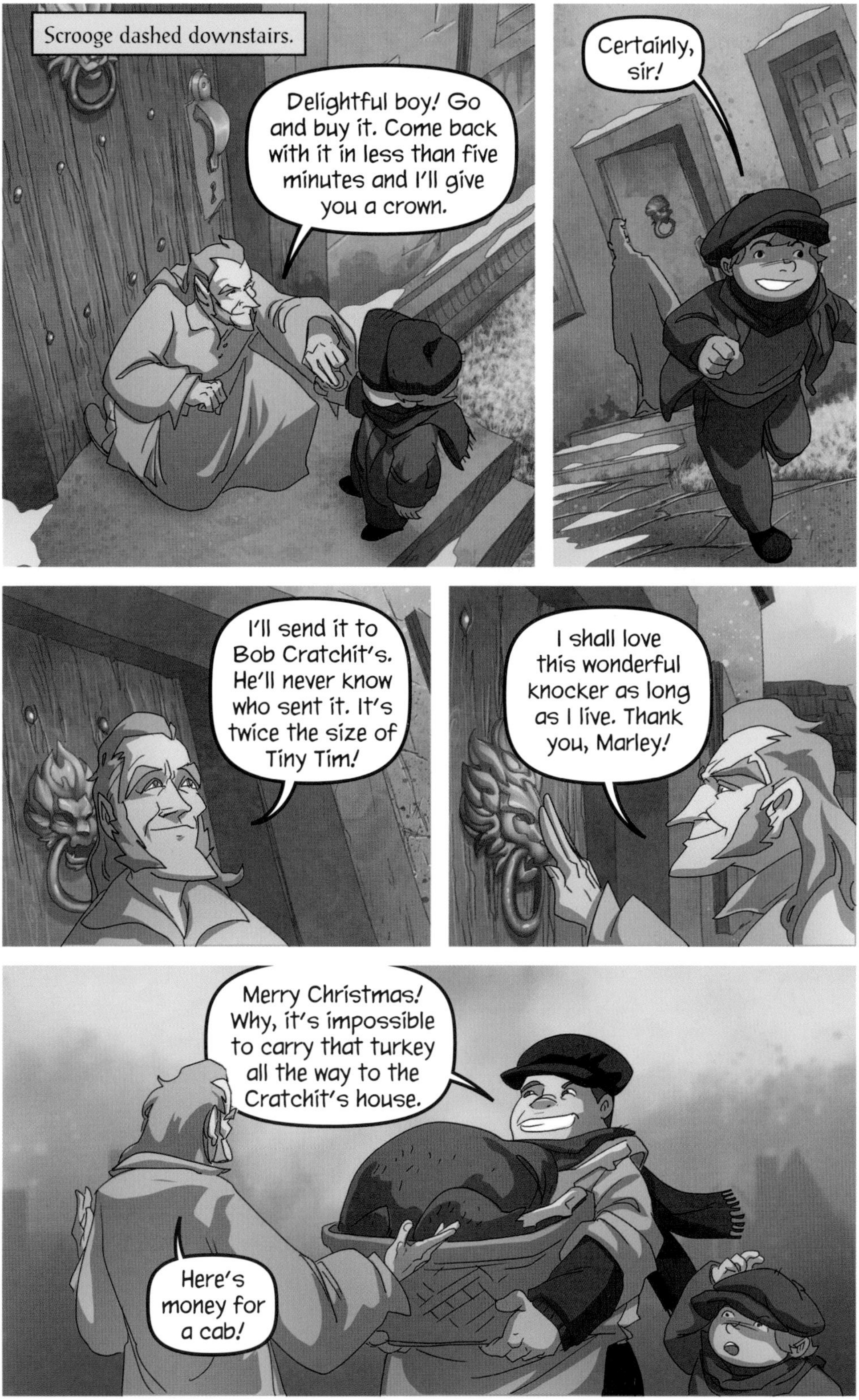
Scrooge dashed downstairs.
Delightful boy! Go and buy it. Come back with it in less than five minutes and I'll give you a crown.
Certainly, sir!
I'll send it to Bob Cratchit's. He'll never know who sent it. It's twice the size of Tiny Tim!
I shall love this wonderful knocker as long as I live. Thank you, Marley!
Merry Christmas! Why, it's impossible to carry that turkey all the way to the Cratchit's house.
Here's money for a cab!

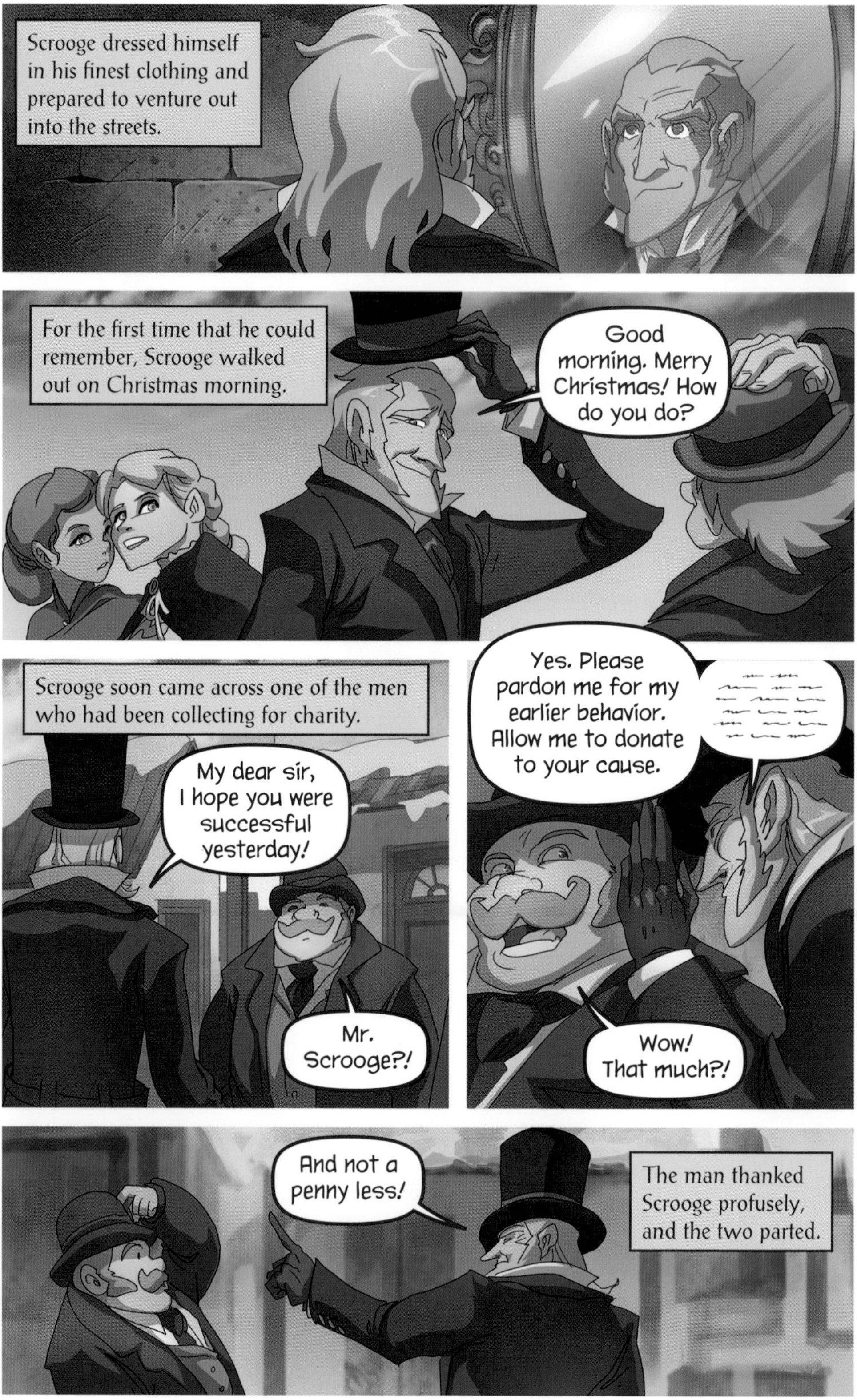
Scrooge dressed himself in his finest clothing and prepared to venture out into the streets.
For the first time that he could remember, Scrooge walked out on Christmas morning.
Good morning. Merry Christmas! How do you do?
Scrooge soon came across one of the men who had been collecting for charity.
My dear sir, I hope you were successful yesterday!
Mr. Scrooge?!
Yes. Please pardon me for my earlier behavior. Allow me to donate to your cause.
Wow! That much?!
And not a penny less!
The man thanked Scrooge profusely, and the two parted.

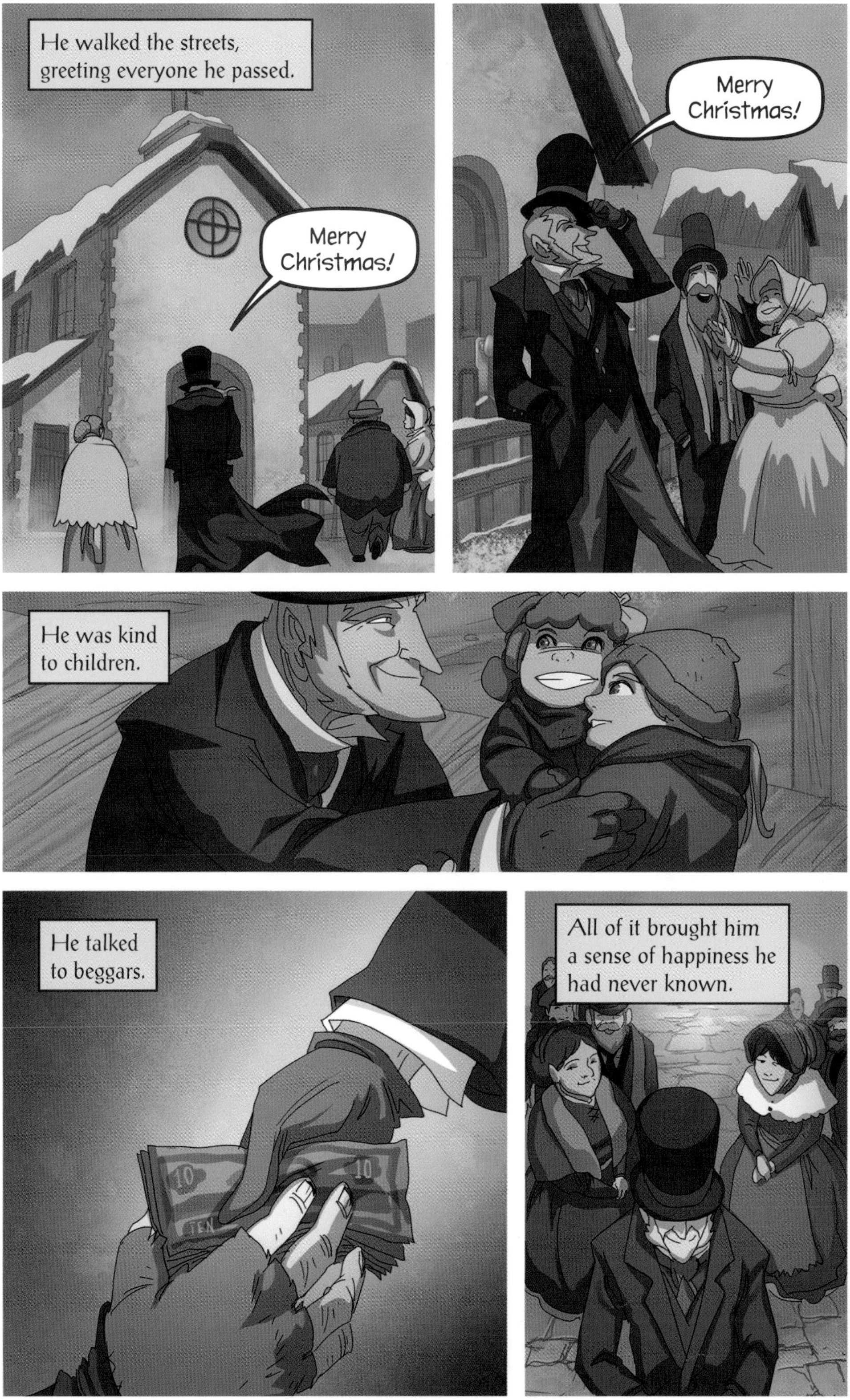
He walked the streets, greeting everyone he passed.
Merry Christmas!
Merry Christmas!
He was kind to children.
He talked to beggars.
10
10
All of it brought him a sense of happiness he had never known.

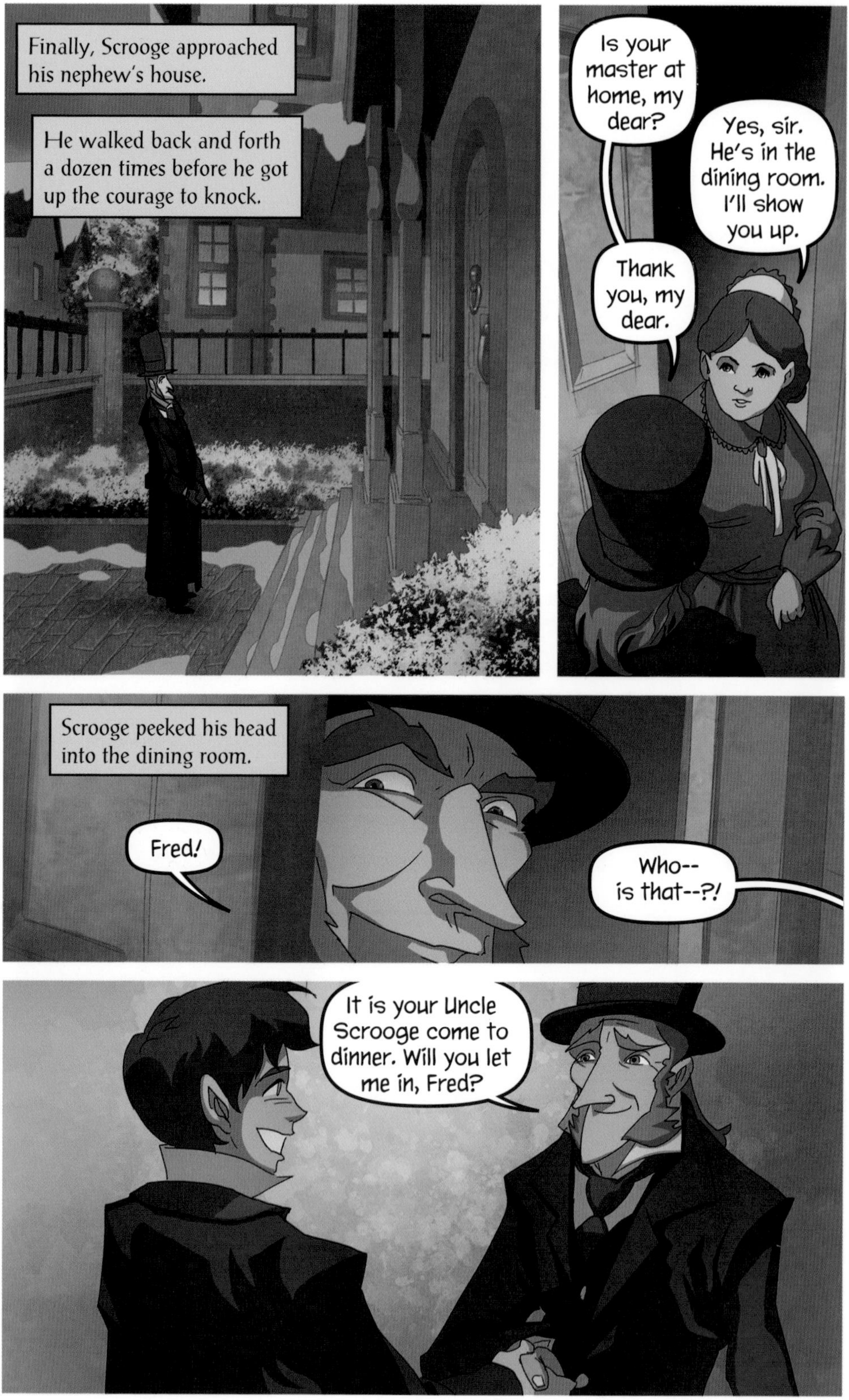
Finally, Scrooge approached his nephew's house.
He walked back and forth a dozen times before he got up the courage to knock.
Is your master at home, my dear?
Yes, sir. He's in the dining room. I'll show you up.
Thank you, my dear.
Scrooge peeked his head into the dining room.
Fred!
Who-- is that--?!
It is your Uncle Scrooge come to dinner. Will you let me in, Fred?

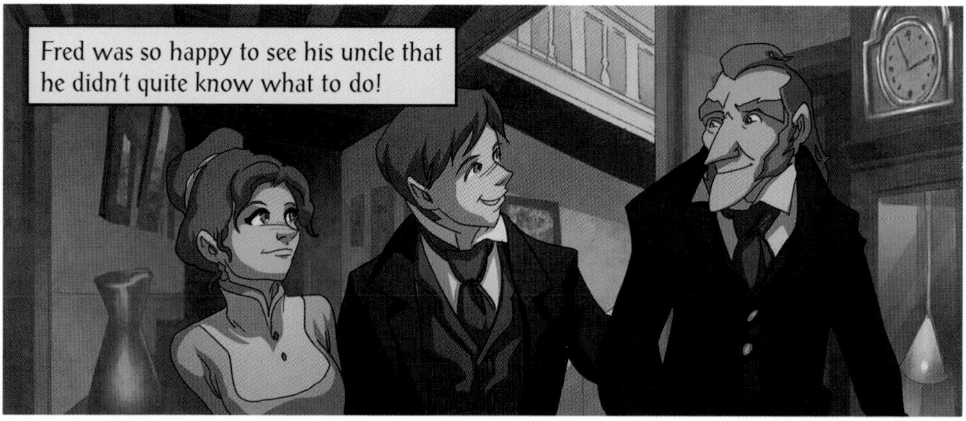
Fred was so happy to see his uncle that he didn't quite know what to do!

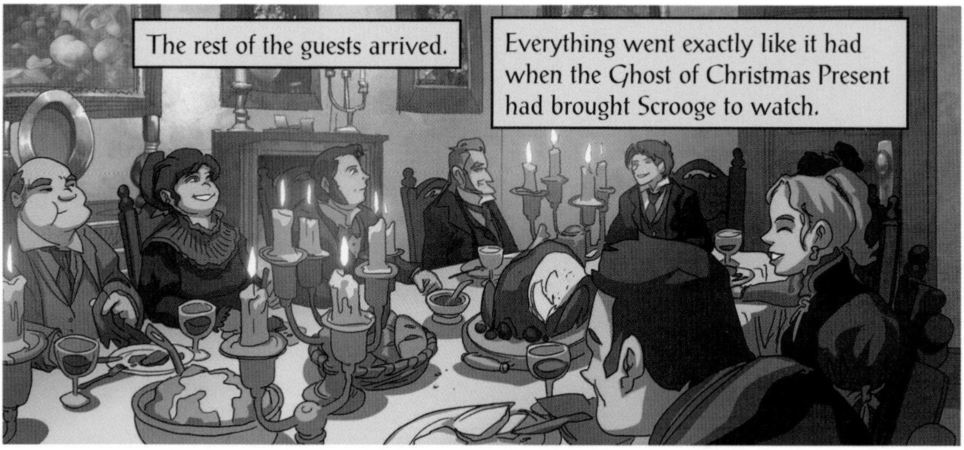
The rest of the guests arrived.
Everything went exactly like it had when the Ghost of Christmas Present had brought Scrooge to watch.

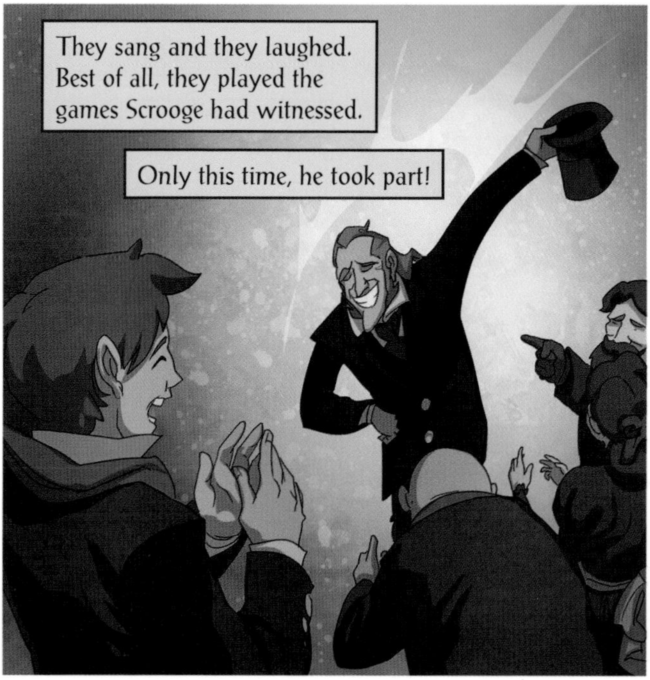
They sang and they laughed. Best of all, they played the games Scrooge had witnessed.
Only this time, he took part!

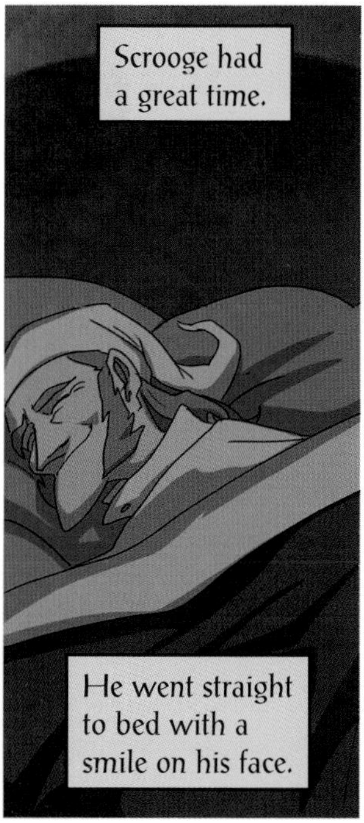
Scrooge had a great time.
He went straight to bed with a smile on his face.

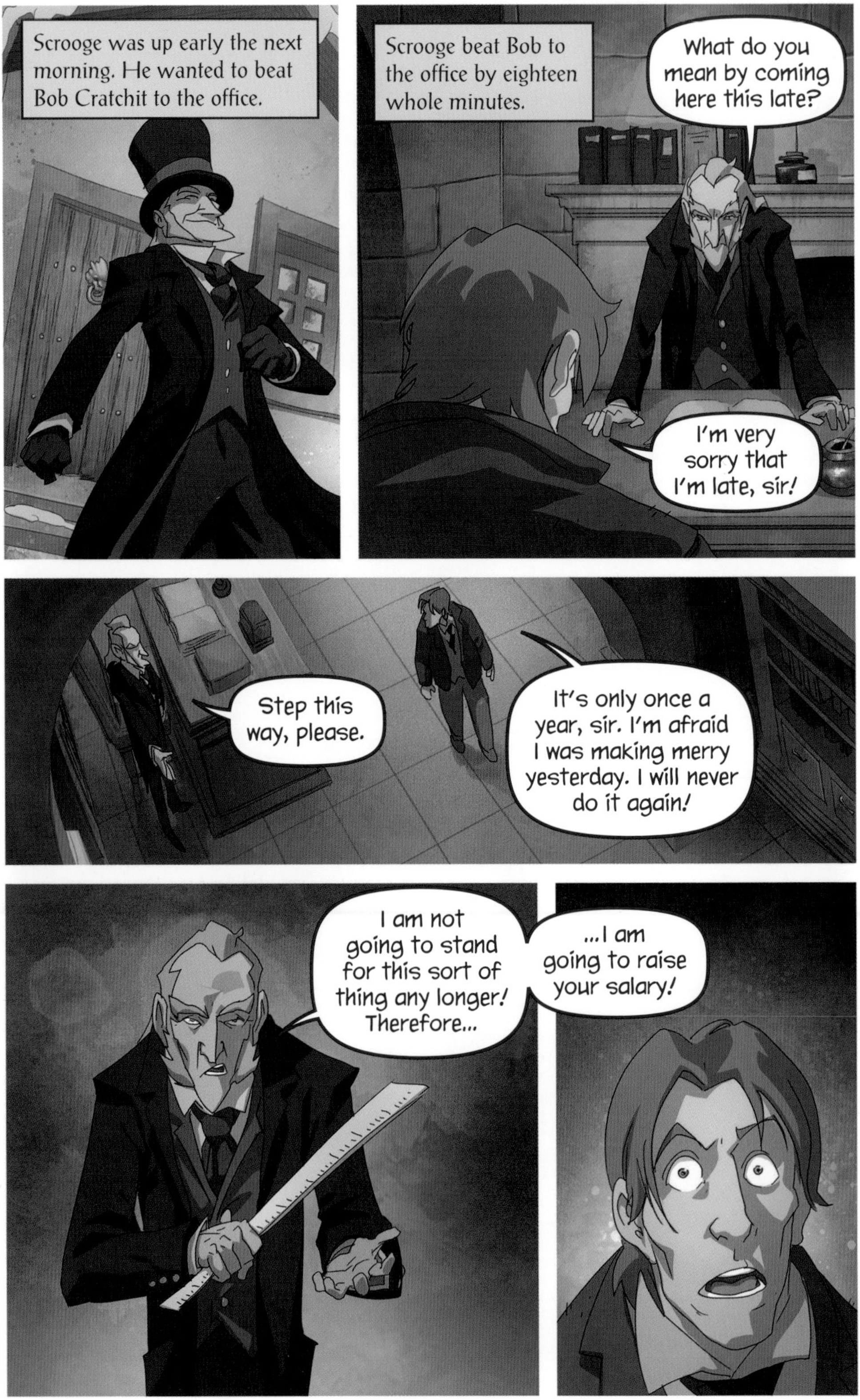
Scrooge was up early the next morning. He wanted to beat Bob Cratchit to the office.
Scrooge beat Bob to the office by eighteen whole minutes.
What do you mean by coming here this late?
I'm very sorry that I'm late, sir!
Step this way, please.
It's only once a year, sir. I'm afraid I was making merry yesterday. I will never do it again!
I am not going to stand for this sort of thing any longer! Therefore...
...I am going to raise your salary!

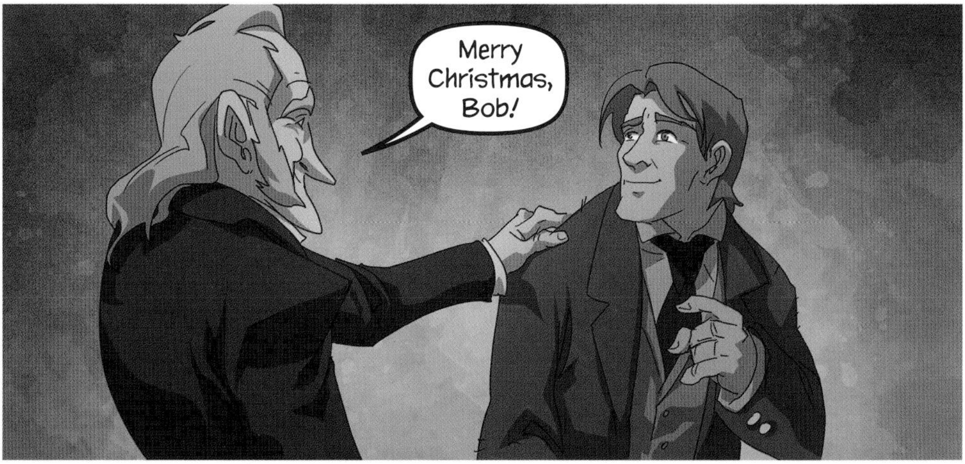
Merry Christmas, Bob!

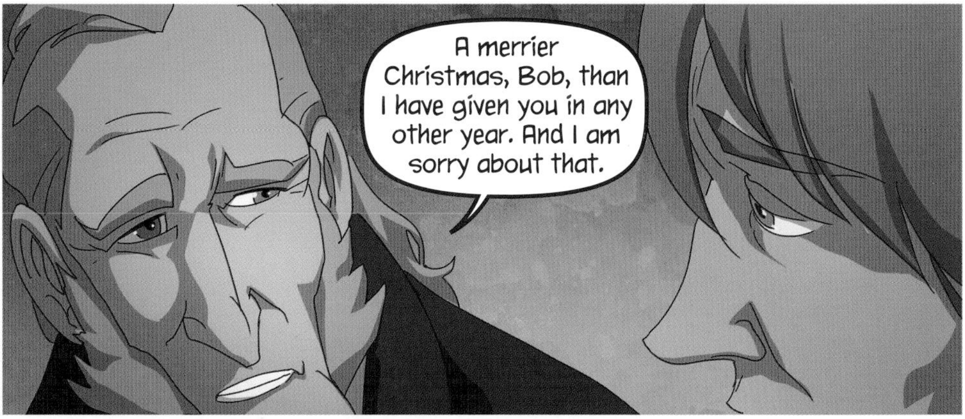
A merrier Christmas, Bob, than I have given you in any other year. And I am sorry about that.

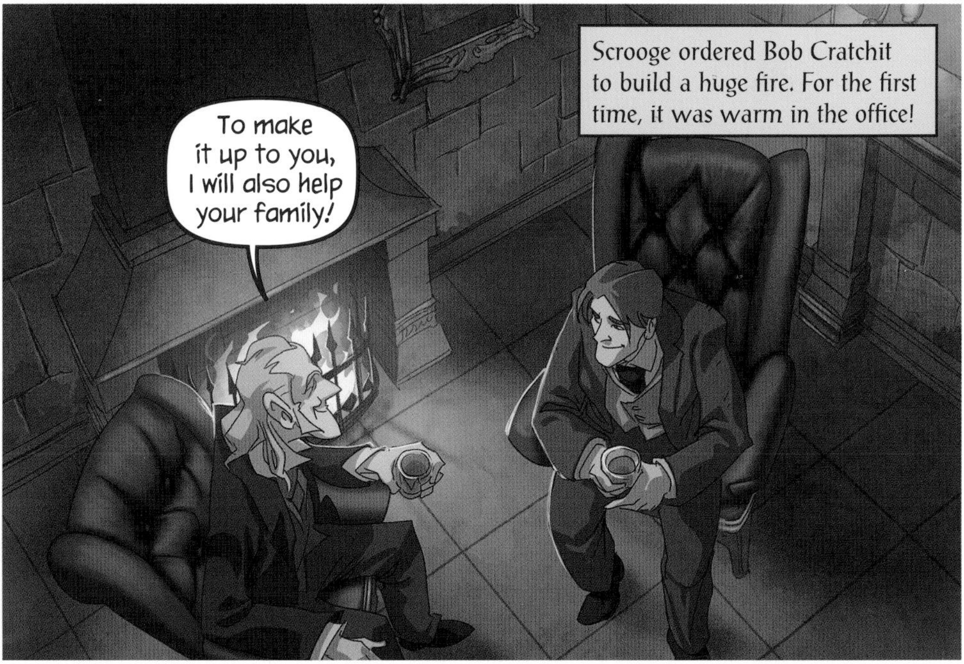
Scrooge ordered Bob Cratchit to build a huge fire. For the first time, it was warm in the office!
To make it up to you, I will also help your family!

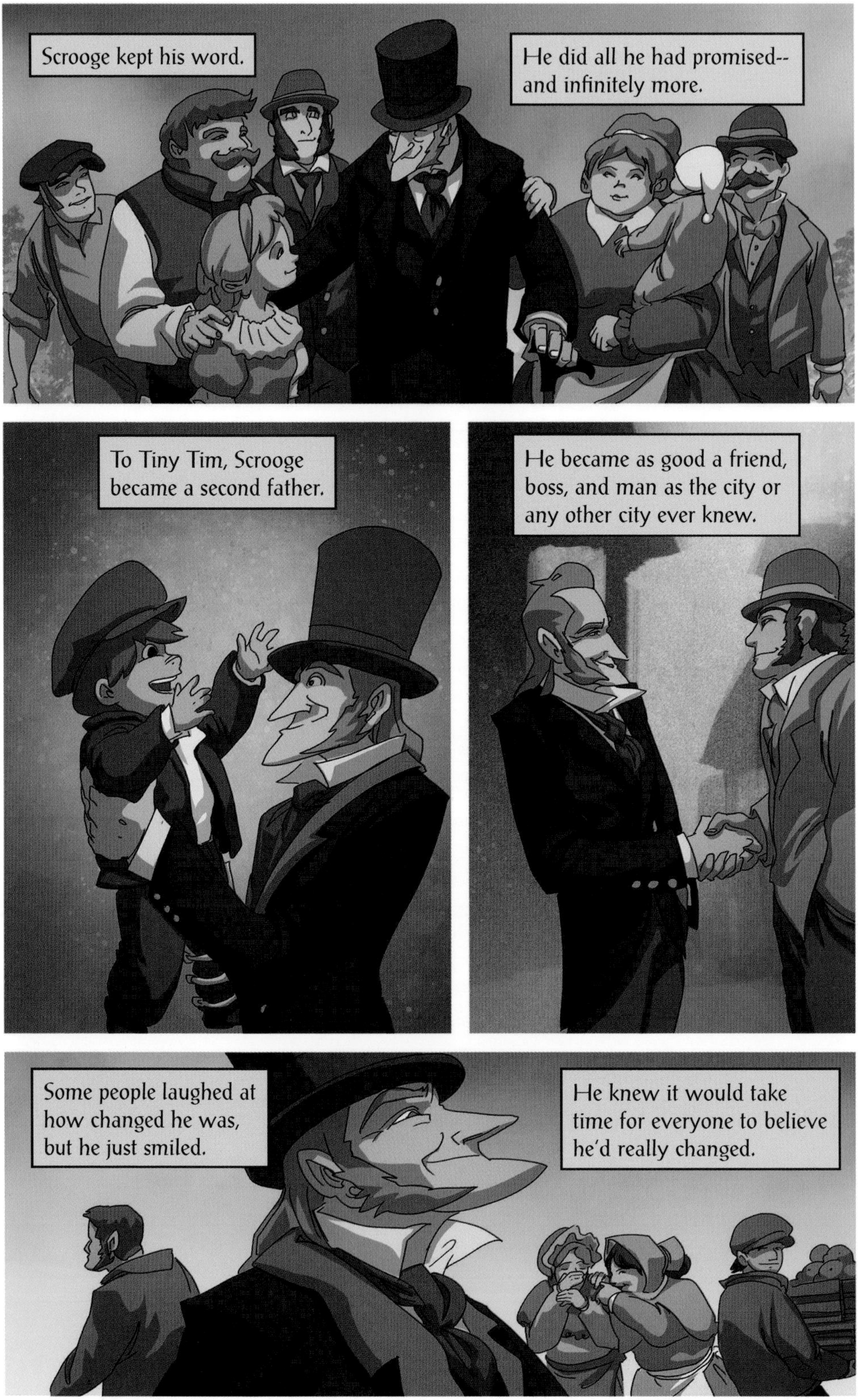
Scrooge kept his word.
He did all he had promised--and infinitely more.
To Tiny Tim, Scrooge became a second father.
He became as good a friend, boss, and man as the city or any other city ever knew.
Some people laughed at how changed he was, but he just smiled.
He knew it would take time for everyone to believe he'd really changed.

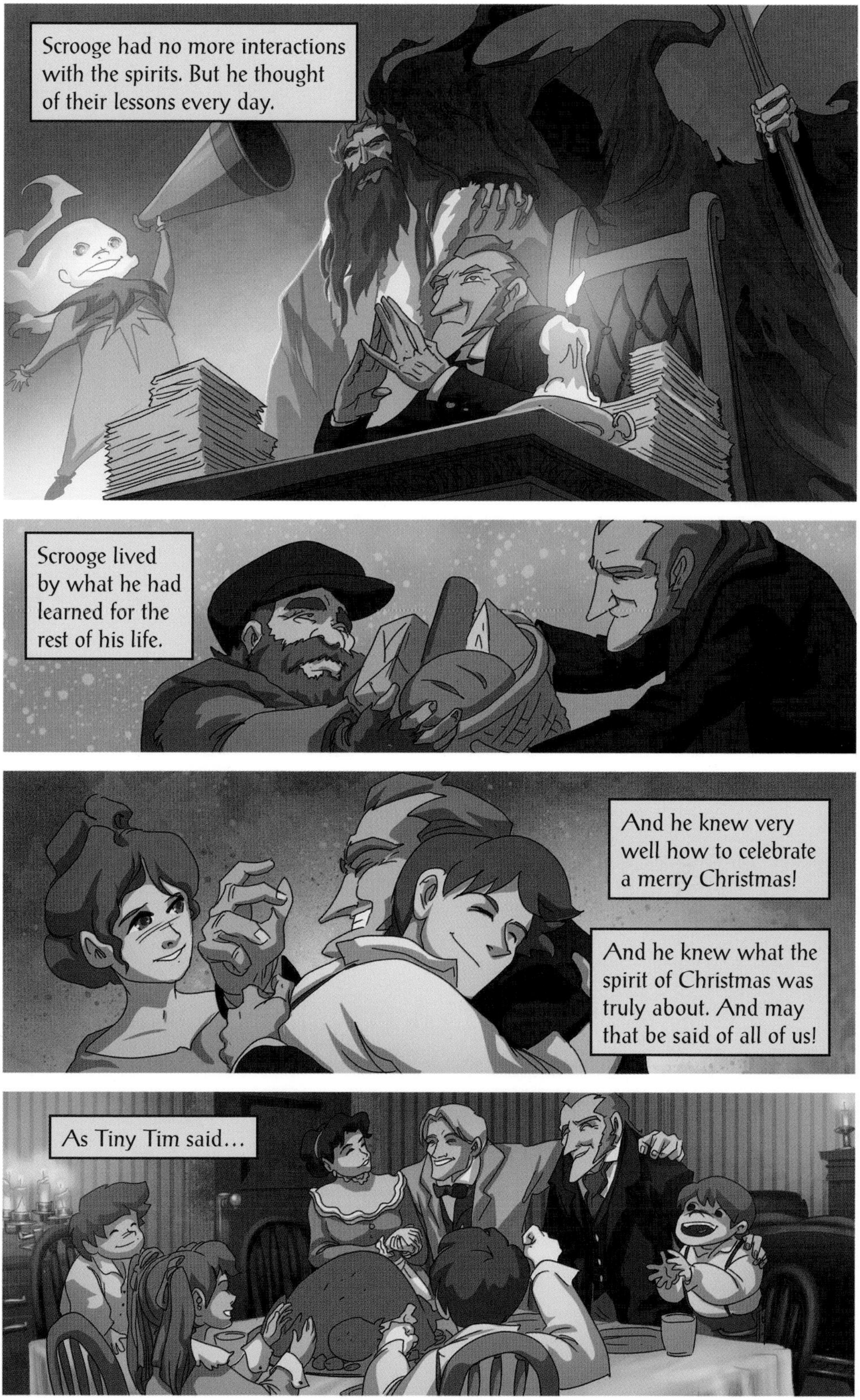
Scrooge had no more interactions with the spirits. But he thought of their lessons every day.
Scrooge lived by what he had learned for the rest of his life.
And he knew very well how to celebrate a merry Christmas!
And he knew what the spirit of Christmas was truly about. And may that be said of all of us!
As Tiny Tim said…

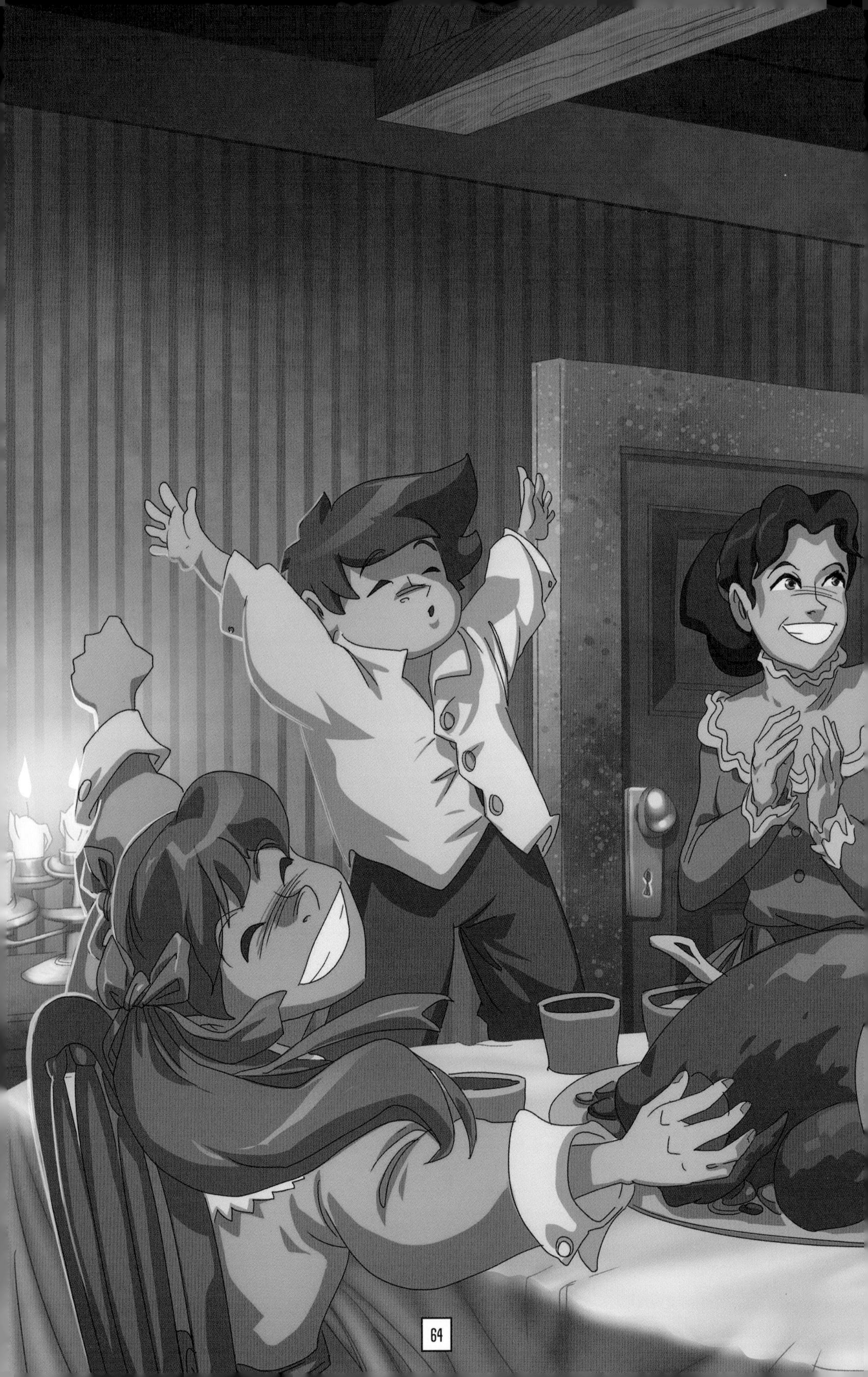

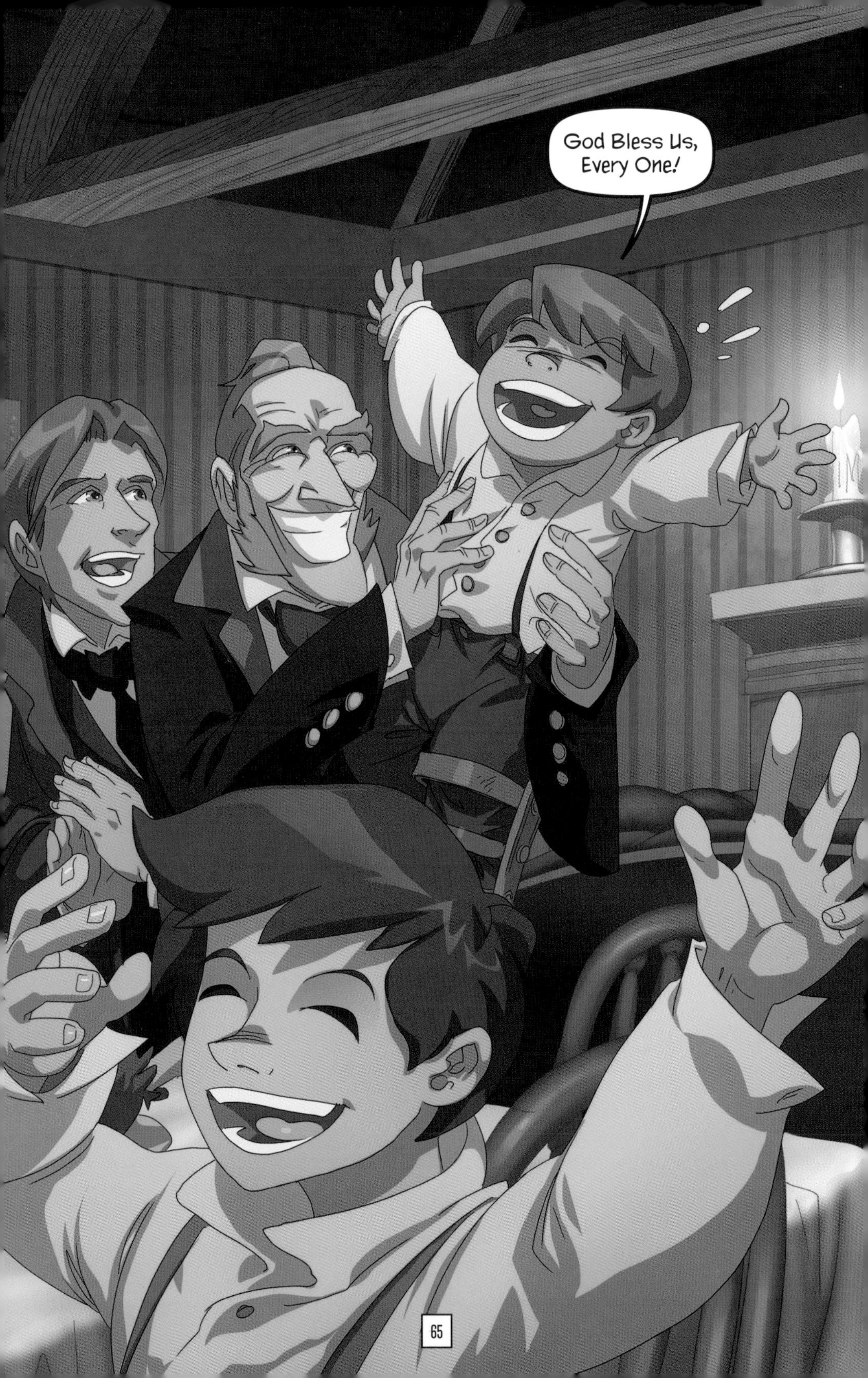
God Bless Us, Every One!

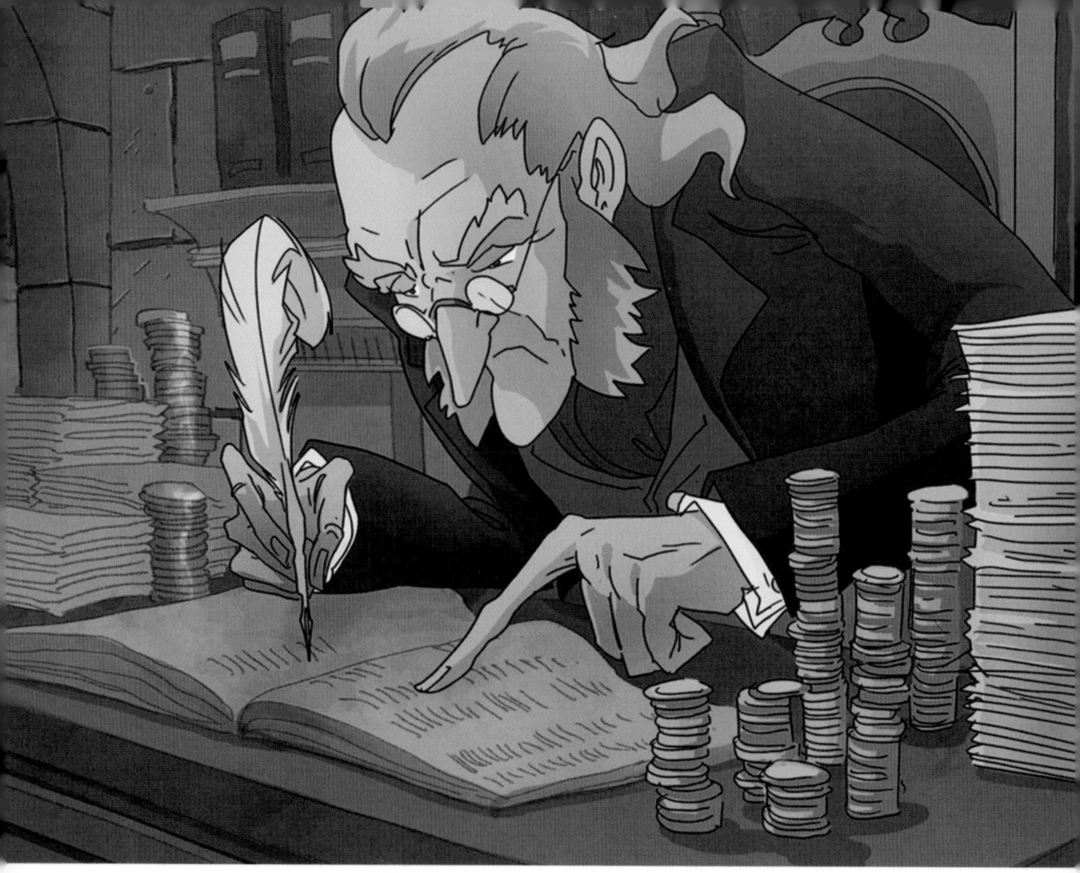

ABOUT THE RETELLING AUTHOR AND ILLUSTRATOR

Benjamin Harper has worked as an editor at Lucasfilm LTD and DC Comics. He currently works at Warner Bros Consumer Products in California. He has written many books, including *Obsessed with Star Wars* and *Thank You, Superman!*

Daniel Perez was born in Monterrey, Mexico, in 1977. For more than a decade, Perez has worked as a colorist and an illustrator for comic book publishers, including Marvel, Image, and Dark Horse.

GLOSSARY

apparition (ap-uh-RISH-uhn)—a ghost or spirit of a dead person

ascended (uh-SEND-id)—climbed or walked upward

convenient (kuhn-VEEN-yuhnt)—allowing you to do something or reach somewhere easily or without trouble

despair (di-SPAYR)—the feeling of no longer having any hope

dismal (DIZ-muhl)—very bad, poor, or not at all cheerful

doomed (DOOMD)—destined to fail or come to ruin

exhausted (ig-ZAHSS-tid)—completely worn out or tired

gloom (GLOOM)—partial or total darkness, or a general feeling of sadness

humbug (HUMM-bug)—language or behavior that is false or deceitful

phantoms (FAN-tuhmz)— the ghosts of dead people

COMMON CORE ALIGNED
READING QUESTIONS

1. The first time you meet Ebenezer Scrooge, what do you learn about Mr. Scrooge? *("Analyze how and why individuals, events, and ideas develop and interact over the course of a text.")*

2. Three significant spirits visit Mr. Scrooge on Christmas Eve. What are the spirits' names? Why did each spirit visit Mr. Scrooge? *("Read closely to determine what the text says explicitly and to make logical inferences from it; cite specific textual evidence when writing or speaking to support conclusions drawn from the text.")*

3. At the end of the text, Mr. Scrooge has learned a few lessons from the spirits. What has he learned, and what does he do about it after the spirits are gone on Christmas Day? *("Read and comprehend complex literary and informational texts independently and proficiently.")*

COMMON CORE ALIGNED
WRITING PROMPTS

1. What would you do if you had Ebenezer Scrooge's money? Would you donate it to charity? Save it? Go on a vacation? Write a family member or friend a letter explaining what you'd do with the money. (*"Write arguments to support claims in an analysis of substantive topics or texts, using valid reasoning and relevant and sufficient evidence."*)

2. In three separate paragraphs, explain why you think each spirit visits Mr. Scrooge. (*"Produce clear and coherent writing in which the development, organization, and style are appropriate to task, purpose, and audience."*)

3. If you could write an email or letter to Mr. Scrooge, what would you want to say to him and why? (*"Produce clear and coherent writing in which the development, organization, and style are appropriate to task, purpose, and audience."*)

READ THEM ALL!

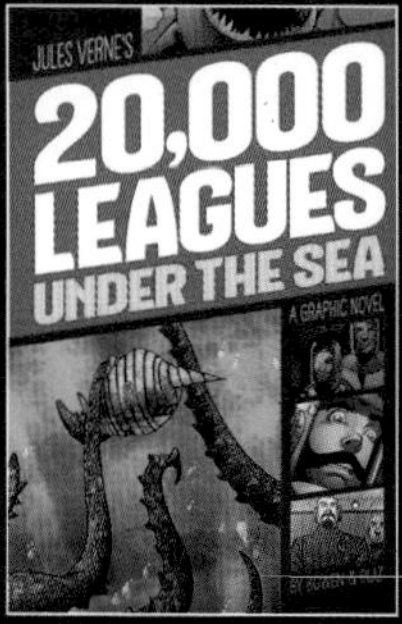
JULES VERNE'S
20,000 LEAGUES UNDER THE SEA
A GRAPHIC NOVEL

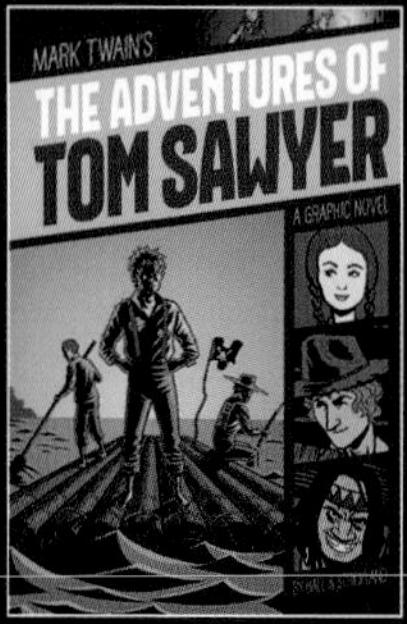
MARK TWAIN'S
THE ADVENTURES OF TOM SAWYER
A GRAPHIC NOVEL

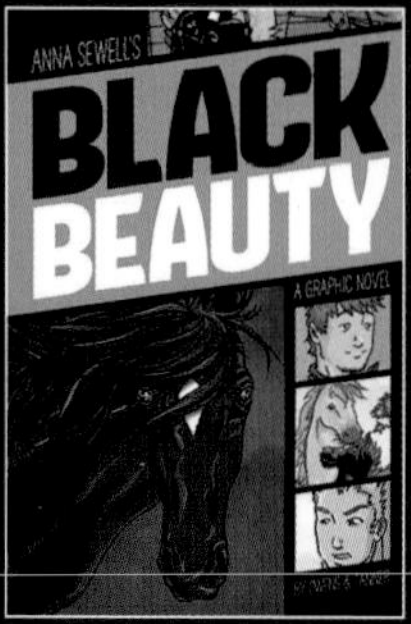
ANNA SEWELL'S
BLACK BEAUTY
A GRAPHIC NOVEL

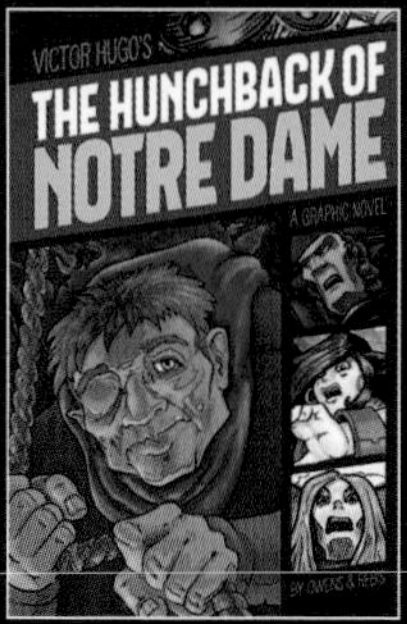
VICTOR HUGO'S
THE HUNCHBACK OF NOTRE DAME
A GRAPHIC NOVEL

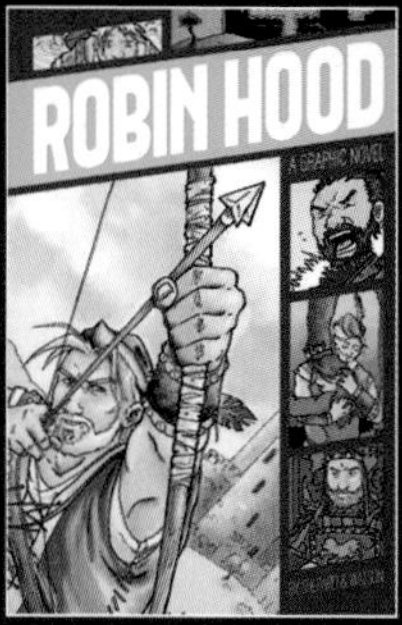
ROBIN HOOD
A GRAPHIC NOVEL

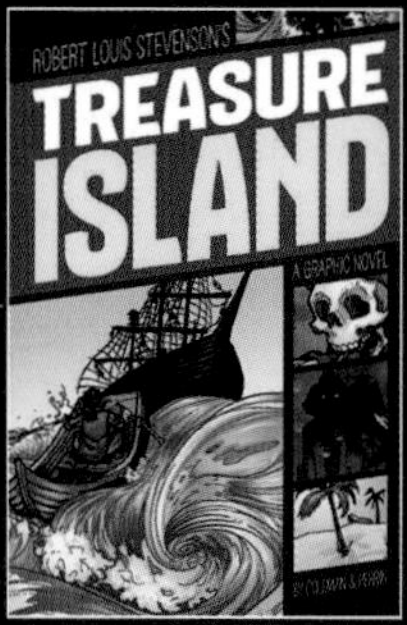
ROBERT LOUIS STEVENSON'S
TREASURE ISLAND
A GRAPHIC NOVEL

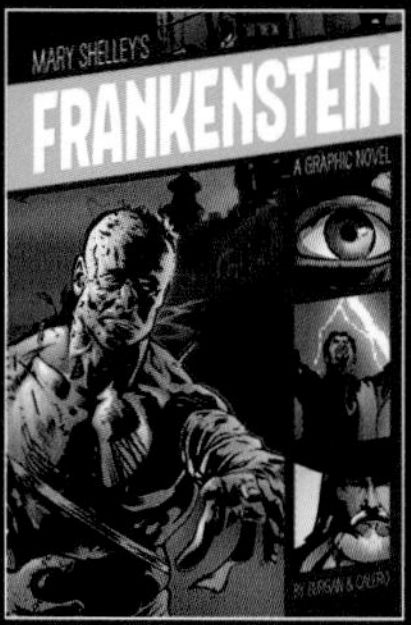
MARY SHELLEY'S
FRANKENSTEIN
A GRAPHIC NOVEL

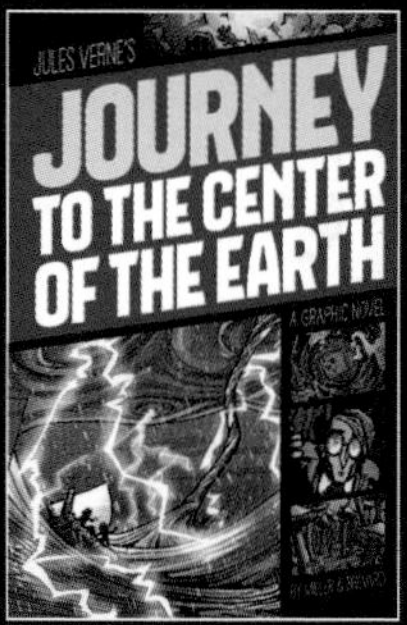
JULES VERNE'S
JOURNEY TO THE CENTER OF THE EARTH
A GRAPHIC NOVEL

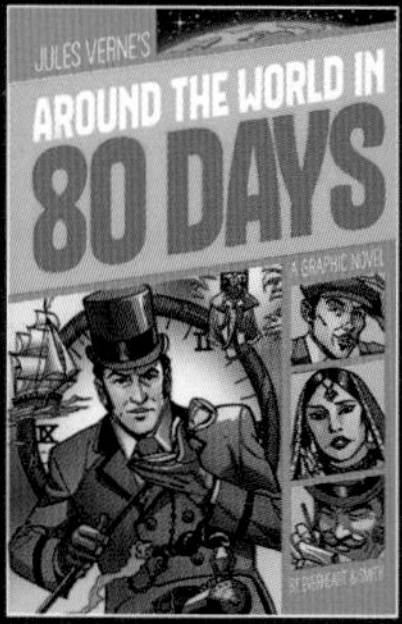
JULES VERNE'S
AROUND THE WORLD IN 80 DAYS
A GRAPHIC NOVEL

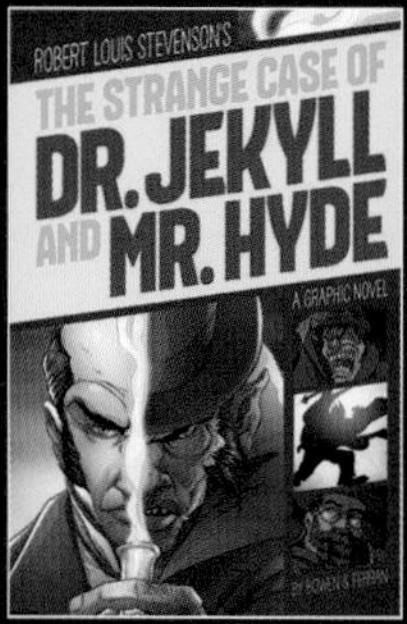
ROBERT LOUIS STEVENSON'S
THE STRANGE CASE OF DR. JEKYLL AND MR. HYDE
A GRAPHIC NOVEL

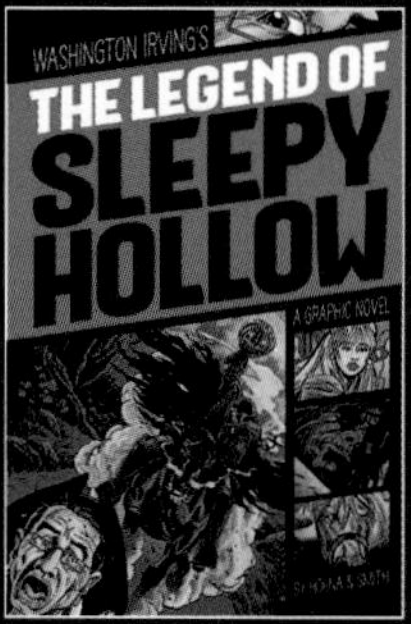
WASHINGTON IRVING'S
THE LEGEND OF SLEEPY HOLLOW
A GRAPHIC NOVEL

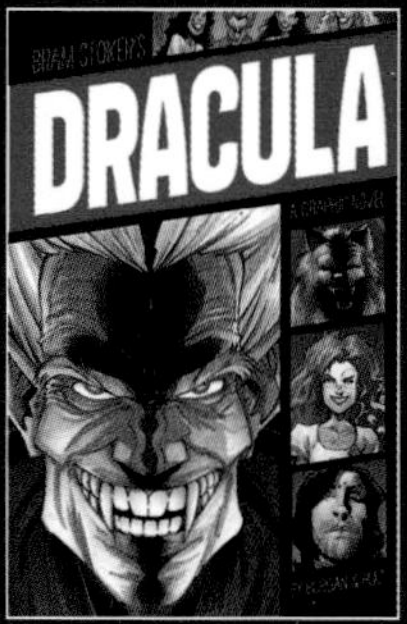
BRAM STOKER'S
DRACULA
A GRAPHIC NOVEL

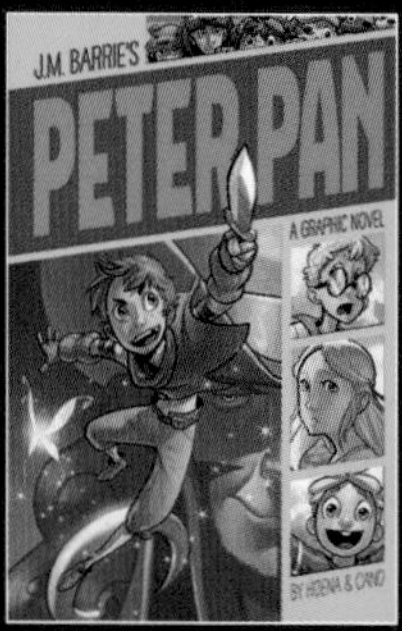
J.M. BARRIE'S
PETER PAN
A GRAPHIC NOVEL

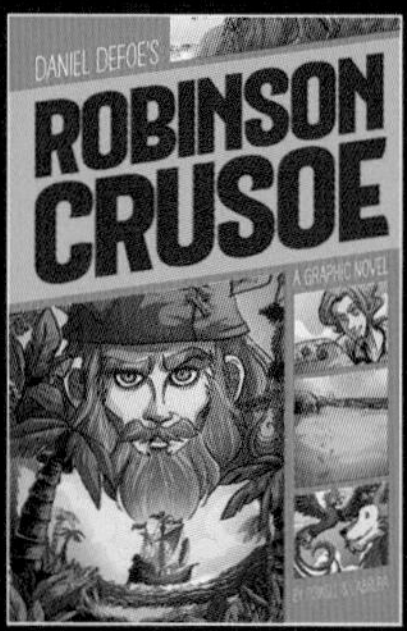
DANIEL DEFOE'S
ROBINSON CRUSOE
A GRAPHIC NOVEL

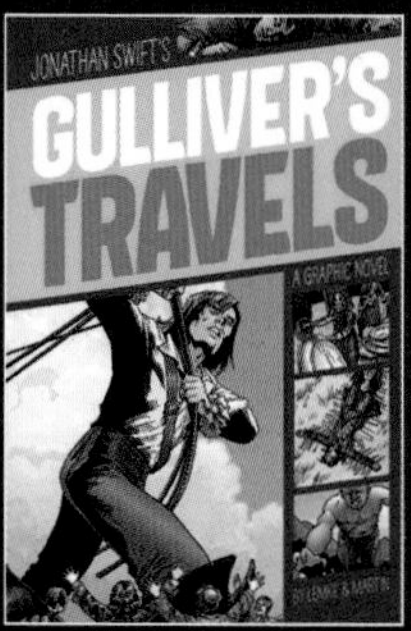
JONATHAN SWIFT'S
GULLIVER'S TRAVELS
A GRAPHIC NOVEL

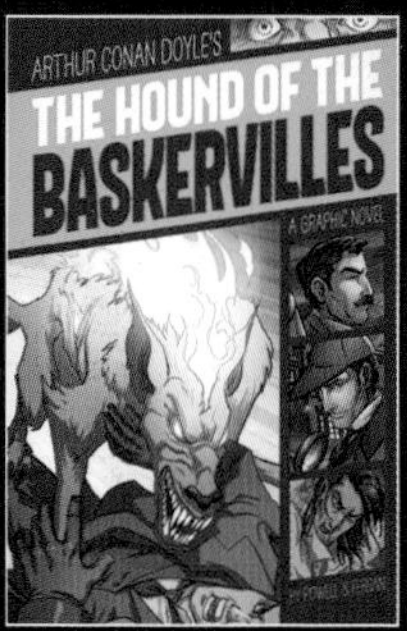
ARTHUR CONAN DOYLE'S
THE HOUND OF THE BASKERVILLES
A GRAPHIC NOVEL

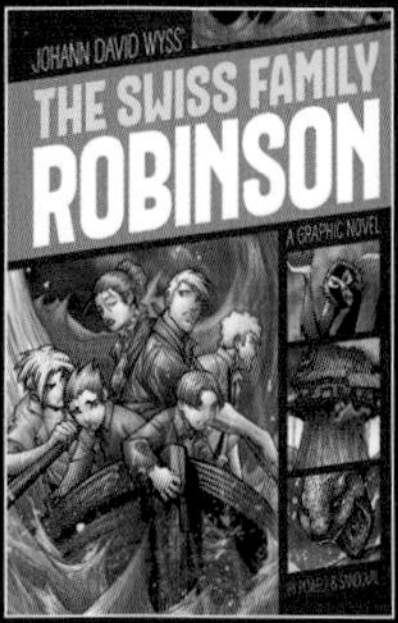
JOHANN DAVID WYSS'
THE SWISS FAMILY ROBINSON
A GRAPHIC NOVEL

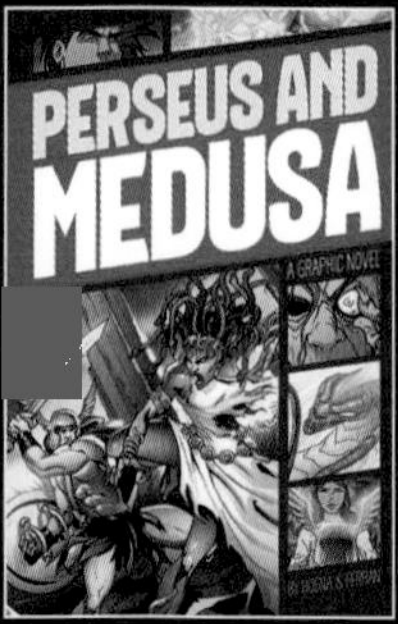
PERSEUS AND MEDUSA
A GRAPHIC NOVEL

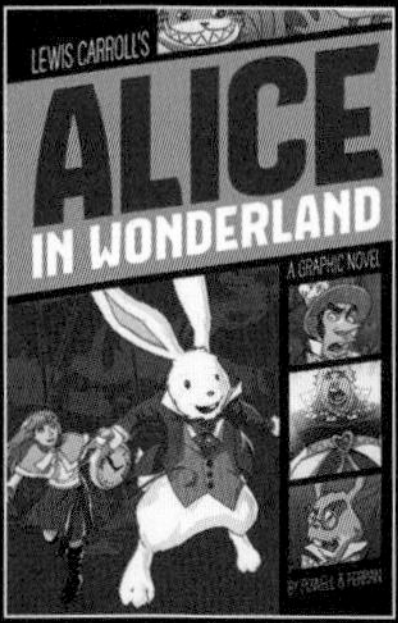
LEWIS CARROLL'S
ALICE IN WONDERLAND
A GRAPHIC NOVEL

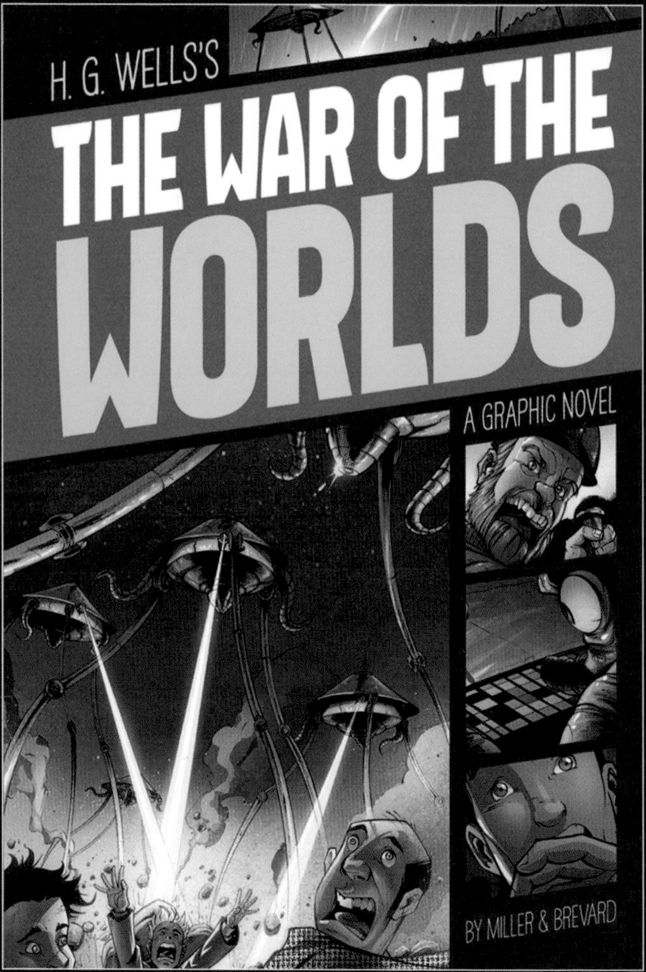
H. G. WELLS'S
THE WAR OF THE WORLDS
A GRAPHIC NOVEL
BY MILLER & BREVARD

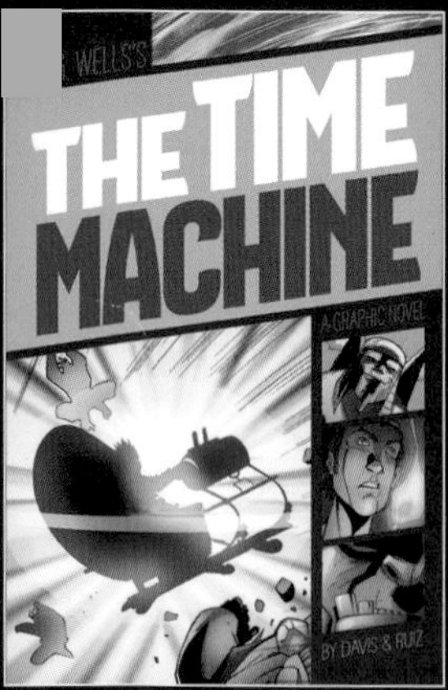
THE TIME MACHINE
A GRAPHIC NOVEL
BY DAVIS & RUIZ

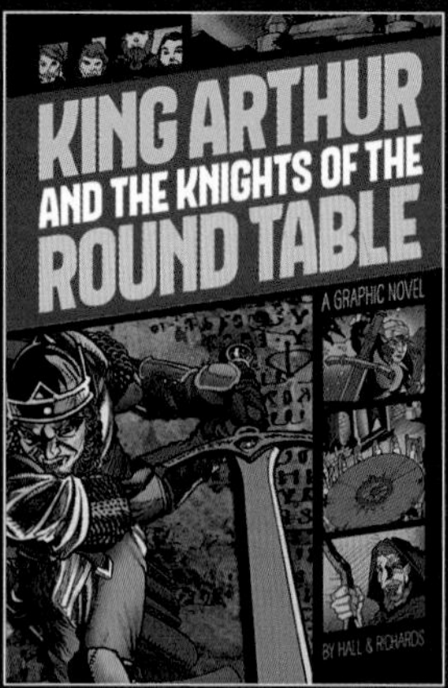
KING ARTHUR AND THE KNIGHTS OF THE ROUND TABLE
A GRAPHIC NOVEL
BY HALL & RICHARDS

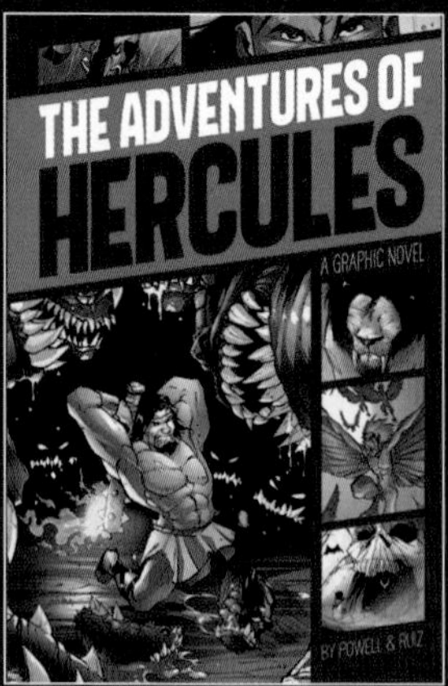
THE ADVENTURES OF HERCULES
A GRAPHIC NOVEL
BY POWELL & RUIZ